SCOUT'S REDEMPTION

Joanne Salemink

Cover design by: Robyn Hepker, Benson-Hepker Designs
Library of Congress Control Number: 2018675309
Printed in the United States of America

Here's to strong women. May we know them.
May we be them. May we raise them.
May we be wise enough to get the heck out of their way
and let them do their thing!

CONTENTS

PROLOGUE

Or

A Brief Recap of
Who's Who and What's What

Once upon a time in the late 1980s, when the hair was bigger, and the music was better, a beautiful (okay, above average looking), orphaned princess/waitress and a handsome, talented musician/prince fell in love. But before things could get interesting, a tricksy ogre named Gary put a curse on Princess Julie and Prince Joe, causing each of them to think the other had dumped them.

The curse lasted for nearly twenty-five years, during which time Princess Julie married the ogre (who turned out to be your average, opportunistic, self-absorbed cad), and together they raised a little princess of their own (who only exhibited the mildest of ogre-like tendencies during her teenage years, as do most teens).

Prince Joe, in the meantime, set out on a quest to prove to Princess Julie he could make something of himself as a musician, and, as luck would have it, ended up becoming a world-famous rock star. He fell under the spell of the sorceress Sophia (that's So-FIE-ah), who may or may not have been evil, but who was certainly a royal pain.

Then one day, the ogre overplayed his hand, and Princess Julie found out he had been sleeping with several fair maidens in the kingdom (including Vanessa, Princess Julie's BFF and lady-in-waiting, whose own prince charming had left her for a prince charming of *his* own).

Princess Julie fled the suburban royal castle to live in the highest tower of Queen Irene's citadel (actually, it was the apartment above the garage). The queen introduced Princess Julie to Sir Big George, his son Page J.J. and *his* son Squire Trey, keepers of The Scout.

The Scout was a 1941 Indian Sport Scout motorcycle with a magic all her own. Her voluptuous body was the glossy black of the darkest midnight sky, her fender skirts were as white as the purest snow, and her chrome accents sparkled like diamonds.

Princess Julie soon fell under the spell of The Scout. Before you could say "timing advance," Julie realized she had always had the power to take control of her life. She broke the ogre's curse, started her own small business, and rescued Joe from an eternity (or what would have seemed like eternity) as one of Sophia's trophy boyfriends.

You would think after all that, Julie and Joe deserved to live happily ever after, but real life isn't like fairy tales. Real life is filled with obligations and honor, fears and plagues, deceptions and chivalry. And sometimes the hardest dragons to slay are those we conjure ourselves.

Chapter 1

Miss Irene was late for her own party.

Technically, she was late for the final planning meeting for her own party, but still . . . . I had never known her to be late for anything. That is partly because she drives with only slightly more caution than a bat out of hell, and partly because being late would be rude and being rude just isn't in her nature.

"Julie! I need you to focus!"

Another reason Miss Irene wouldn't have intentionally been late to this meeting was because she knew that would leave me stuck alone with Sophia. And that would be cruel. And Miss Irene would never be that cruel to me.

"Julie! Put your phone down! This is important!"

Apparently, the updated old adage is true: A watched phone never rings. It also doesn't shoot a phaser beam that will stun someone into silence. I know, because I pointed my phone at Sophia and whispered "pew-pew" before putting it down, giving up on hearing from Miss Irene, and giving Sophia my full attention.

"You have to talk to Joe about his schedule." Sophia had taken advantage of Miss Irene's tardiness and the resultant hostage situation to harangue me about my boyfriend. "It was hard enough trying to book around his 'do-gooder' work mentoring new bands. Now he's insisting on work-free 'Julie Weekends' to spend with you. It's ridiculous!"

Sophia's rabid-dog tenacity made her invaluable when it came to hammering out contracts, Joe said. Personally, I thought it made her annoying. *Po-tay-to, po-tah-to.*

"Joe's a hot commodity right now. We need to take advantage of that. We need to . . . ."

"That boy's a real talent. He's always gonna be a 'hot commodity'," Bob said gruffly as he brought me a refill of soda and pointedly ignored Sophia's empty glass.

Sophia snorted. "That *boy* is 52. He's riding a wave of baby boomer, Gen Xer nostalgia."

Joe was out in California courting those baby-Xers while I stayed at home babysitting Bob and Sophia. They had gotten off on the wrong foot because . . . well, because Sophia was Sophia. Most of the time, I wanted to strangle her myself.

"*They're* the target audience. *They're* the consumers with disposable income. *They're* the ones buying the tickets. But it can't last forever. All it takes is a couple of broken boomer hips and Bam! Joe goes from headlining at the Hard Rock to playing acoustic sets on the nursing home circuit."

"Tony Bennett. Frank Sinatra. The Rolling Stones. Billy . . . ." Bob brushed aside Sophia's argument by listing performers who continued to draw big, multi-generational audiences late in their careers.

"Clive Angleman. Flamingo Lips. Tassel Surfers. Marion Morrison," she countered.

"Who?"

"My point exactly." Sophia smiled smugly, sat back in her chair and crossed her arms under her bosom.

I doubted the authenticity of her resulting overly abundant cleavage as much as I doubted her parents had actually named her So-*FIE*-ah LeClaire. I suspected her real name was something much more common and fitting, like Susan or Sandy . . . or Satan.

Bob, realizing this was an argument he wouldn't win, scowled at me, then stalked off to the kitchen to check on the lunch special. I didn't know if Sophia was bluffing or not, but he would. As owner of The Bar – *the* home for live music in Pleasant Glen and all of Eastern Iowa – Bob Donnelly had helped launch the careers of many promising bands, including Joe Davenport and The Average Joes. That was back in the late 1980s, when I was a waitress here. This is where Joe and I met, fell in love, and then let fame, fate and pride keep us apart for twenty-five years. Of course "fate" had help from the man who became my lying, cheating, soon-to-be ex-husband, Gary Westbrook.

"I finally convinced Joe to focus on the big picture, career-wise, and then you and your little Gala derailed me. I mean *him*," Sophia said, turning her attention back to me.

The more personal aspects of Sophia's role as Joe's personal manager had been eliminated when Joe and I reconnected a few months ago. Joe assured me it hadn't been anything serious and that he was merely a trophy she showed off when her other three suitors were busy. Sophia seemed to be adjusting well until a certain rich Texas oilman dumped her for a younger model. This was impressive, given that Sophia herself was twenty years younger than Mr. RTO.

"Volunteerism may be good for Joe's image, but it doesn't pay the bills." Sophia continued to talk as she pulled my glass across the table, put her straw in it, and took a long drink. She looked up at me, mouth full of *my* soda, and batted her eyelids in a thoroughly unconvincing display of innocence. She then tilted the glass towards me as if to ask if I'd like a drink – *of my own soda.*

I'm not afraid of a little backwash. I had raised a child, I had dealt with floaters. But I wasn't sure which antibiotic – or antivenom – would counteract whatever Sophia might have left behind in the glass. I shook my head, declining the offer.

"All this benevolent bull crap gives me the heebie jeebies," she shuddered. "Not that there's anything inherently wrong with rescuing orphaned wombats. It's just that those of us with *real* jobs have more important – and interesting – things to do with our time. What did you say your charity *du jour* was?"

"I'm helping organize the wombat . . . I mean the animal shelter's adoption carnival."

"Adoption carnival?" Sophia sounded genuinely interested, which unnerved me. "I've always wanted a dalmatian . . . give or take a hundred." Her Cruella deVil-like cackle unnerved me even more.

I was used to Sophia's obnoxious behavior. It was her seemingly benign comments that bothered me. My current "real job" as an event coordinator had evolved from my "do-gooder work." For years, I had organized galas, fundraisers and classroom parties for various Pleasant Glen clubs, churches and schools. Now I hoped to turn that into a business. It wasn't rocket surgery or brain science, but it kept me busy – busy enough that I couldn't just rush off to join Joe at the drop of an airline ticket.

Between my schedule and Joe's schedule – which had been set months ago, prior to "work-free Julie weekends" – we didn't get to spend as much time together as we'd like. It was not the most ideal way to rekindle a romance begun so long ago, but we were making the best of it.

Take this weekend, for example. Although we were half a country apart, we were coordinating to work on the same project. Sort of. I – at Joe's urging – was keeping Bob and Sophia from killing each other. Sophia – at Joe's urging – had agreed to manage the career of Six-On-Six, an all-girl band from nearby Mediapolis he was mentoring. Bob – at Joe's urging – had booked Six-On-Six to perform at The Bar. And finally, I was using the band's performance as the centerpiece of Miss Irene's bachelorette party.

It was a winning situation all around, especially for Miss Irene. She had been a starting forward on the 1942 Pleasant Glen High School girls basketball team that was stopped one game short of the state tournament by a scrappy Wilton Junction squad. She had fond memories of the six-player style of play and knew all the words to Six-On-Six's hit song, "Dribble, Dribble, Shoot."

An up-and-coming band performing at The Bar wasn't anything unusual, but a bachelorette party was. Bob had outlawed all wedding-related gatherings years ago, after a drunken bridesmaid had nearly clocked Joe with a contraband champagne bottle. A plucky waitress – me – saved Joe from a certain concussion by tackling the overzealous fan as she rushed the stage. Muffy still harbored a grudge.

The early bird lunch crowd started to trickle in as Bob, Sophia and I finished going over last-minute details for the party.

"Just make sure everyone keeps their clothes on," Bob said, "especially Miss Irene." Sophia nearly choked on her . . . I mean *my* . . . soda when she heard that. *Thank you karma.*

Technically, Miss Irene had been practicing *pole dancing*, not stripping, when she fell and bruised her ego. The Pleasant Glen gossip grapevine didn't bother with such distinctions, given Miss Irene and Big George's prior exploits, which included several moonlit skinny dips that may have contributed to the high turnover rate among the city's lifeguards. Miss Irene's children, who had grown used to the couple's hijinks, were more concerned about her fall than her dance moves and had demanded several safety measures, including hiring a full-time companion – me, again.

Miss Irene quickly became much more than my landlord/employer. She was my mentor, mother-figure, and - at most times - role model. She had also introduced me to The Scout, a beautiful, 1941 Indian Sport Scout motorcycle. Once upon a time, The Scout had brought Miss Irene and Big George together. After fifty years as business partners and friends with benefits – which I tried not to think about – they were finally getting married. Hence the bachelorette party tonight and the meeting this morning.

"Where is the bawdy bride, anyway?" Sophia asked. "Shouldn't she be here making sure there's enough handicapped parking for all the mobility scooters?"

"You'd better hope Miss Irene doesn't hear you making that kind of crack. She'll run you over with her scooter," Bob said as he returned to the bar. "I'll help her."

Miss Irene's children had, indeed, tried to make her replace The Scout with a mobility scooter. The scooter was currently sitting in the garage, gathering dust. The Scout was not.

I checked my watch. "I thought Miss Irene would be here by now. Bob wanted to go over the ground rules with her . . ."

"Clothing is NOT optional," Bob reminded.

"Then we're heading to the airport to pick up her daughter.

6

Miss Irene went to school with Trey this morning . . . something about helping him with a special class assignment. If you ask me, I think she was going to pump him for information about what the boys have planned for Big George's bachelor party." Trey, a senior at Pleasant Glen High School, was Big George's grandson.

Bob shook his head. "Miss Irene in a classroom with a bunch of impressionable young minds. What could go wrong?"

My phone buzzed, as karma rejected my earlier thank you and took Bob's question as a challenge. I scanned the text message and jumped up from the table.

"Hold on! You can't leave her here without adult supervision!" Bob shouted, pointing at Sophia.

"It's an emergency! If she gets out of line, spritz her with the soda gun." I paused in the doorway. "Miss Irene's been sent to the principal's office."

Chapter 2

Not much has changed about Pleasant Glen High School since I graduated from there, more class reunions ago than I like to think about. In fact, not much has changed about the school since it was built in 1975. Spurred by a baby boomlet and an uptick in the economy, Pleasant Glen voters had, uncharacteristically, agreed to pledge years of future taxes to finance an impressive building that was larger, nicer, and better equipped than strictly necessary. Economic fortunes and enrollment had risen and fallen, but careful stewardship kept the building up to date.

Overseeing it all was Miss Marjorie Finestock, school secretary extraordinaire. Miss Finestock, or "Ma'am" – as in "Yes, Ma'am" – has ruled these halls with a firm yet caring hand since the building opened. She inherited her position from her aunt, Gladys Finestock, who had in turn taken over for her aunt, and so forth. Two of the current Miss Finestock's nieces are secretaries at the elementary and junior high buildings, awaiting succession upon her retirement. A multitude of principals and superintendents have been guided, educated, and ultimately fledged to larger school districts by Finestock foremothers.

I rang the bell in the foyer, then waved at the security camera as I waited for the second set of doors to be unlocked. The upgraded security was a recent and sobering change. I entered the main office and found the normally unflappable Miss Finestock looking decidedly flapped. She was repeatedly running her fingers through her short gray hair, leaving distinct furrows.

"About. Damn. Time," she hissed quietly. The only other time I had heard her speak that sharply was when Gilbert Gunderson hoisted Jimmy Vincent's pants up the flagpole – with Jimmy still in them. Miss Finestock made sure Gilly got what he deserved. Then again, I thought Little Jimmy was a twerp, so he did, too.

A window to the right of Miss Finestock's desk overlooked the student commons, and the door to the principal's office was to her left. I heard loud voices arguing behind the closed door.

"Good morning, Ma'am," I said cautiously. "Is Trey . . . ." I pointed at the principal's door.

"Trey is fine, the poor dear. I sent him out to deal with the student uprising."

"The stu . . . ."

"We have a bit of a situation here," she huffed. "Irene was being . . . Irene. She and coach Frieh had a run-in and started fighting like cats in a bag, as they always do. But young Dexter – *Principal* Dexter – decided, unwisely, to make an example of her."

The shouting in the office grew louder.

"I was letting them stew until you got here, hoping he'd recognize a hopeless situation when he saw it, but . . . ."

"*Gol' darn it, Irene!*" I heard Coach shout, followed by a whoop of Miss Irene's laughter.

"In the meantime Dexter contacted the constabulary and . . . ." She paused and looked at a monitor as someone requested admittance. "Oh, dear. They sent Deputy Doug." She shook her head and buzzed him through. "Well, maybe this will work in

9

our favor."

Deputy David Doug was a recent graduate of the police academy and the newest member of the PGPD. He was rumored to have been reduced to tears by Miss Irene during his first day on the job. She had run out of the hair salon – still wearing the beautician's cape – when she saw him ticketing her for parking The Scout in a handicapped parking spot. Doc Houseman had reluctantly approved her for a parking permit after the pole dancing incident. He was not only concerned that she may have suffered a concussion in the fall, but worried she might repeat her performance to prove her competence.

What happened next was unclear. Miss Irene said she accidentally poked Deputy Doug with the official placard she had wedged under the motorcycle's seat. He said she assaulted him with it. Chief Clancy convinced Doug not to press charges. The Chief reasoned that any moral victory gained by enforcing the letter of the law would be lost in the public relations nightmare when it became known Doug claimed a woman less than half his size and nearly four times his age had attacked him with a flimsy plastic card the size of an envelope.

Doug paled when he heard Miss Irene's voice from behind the door.

"Don't faint on me now, Deputy. I'm counting on you to do the right thing." Miss Finestock lowered her chin and looked at Doug over the top of her oversized glasses. It was the same look she used to maintain order in the halls of PGHS.

After summoning her assistant from the copy room, Miss Finestock knocked on the principal's door and – without waiting for an answer – led us in. Miss Irene and Coach Frieh were seated in chairs at opposite ends of the principal's desk. The principal sat behind his desk, facing the door, sipping from a bottle of antacid.

"Principal Dexter, you know Deputy Doug." The young officer nodded at Dexter, then stood behind the coach. "And this is Julie Westbrook, Miss Irene's . . . legal guardian." I took my place behind Miss Irene.

"Good gracious, Miss Irene! First you shanghai poor Trey into your motorized mayhem, and now little Julie, here? Have you no shame, woman?" Butch Frieh was not only the winningest coach in PGHS history, he was also the longest serving, which may have explained the "winningest" part. He and Miss Finestock had joined the staff at the same time, and he had been my high school government teacher.

"Miss Finestock, I told you and Trey I could handle this on my own," Miss Irene said crossly.

"You told us not to call Big George. You didn't mention Julie."

"Then why is *he* here?" Irene nodded her head toward the office door, where Big George now stood.

The "Big" in "Big George" referenced his position as the senior of three generations of Georges, which included J.J. – George Junior, and Trey – George III. "Big" George wasn't actually "big" physically. He was built like a wrestler, short and wiry. But standing there arms akimbo, he seemed to fill the doorway.

"There you are, my dear," he said, smiling at Miss Irene. I saw a familiar twinkle in his brown eyes and knew he was up to something. "You're trending on the Twitter!" Big George swiped his finger across the screen of his smart phone, then handed it to her.

"Pound sign 'Free Irene'?" she read aloud. Principal Dexter took another drink of antacid.

"J.J.'s back at the shop fielding calls from the media. And setting up appointments for scooter maintenance," Big George said.

"What does that have to do with us being here?" I asked.

Miss Irene, Coach Frieh and Principal Dexter all began talking at once, each eager to tell their side of the story. Miss Finestock took control, moderating a semi-coherent explanation of the morning's events.

"Trey and his buddies pimped my ride!" Miss Irene crowed. "They worked on my mobility scooter all summer as an independent study project for automotive class. Today was their big reveal."

"Yes. As I'm sure you know, we here at PGHS are quite proud of the outstanding work being done in our STEM classes, namely science, technology, engineering, and mathematics." I resisted the urge to thank Principal Dexter for mansplaining that to me. "Mr. Dretti has done an excellent job of integrating work-place learning situations into his curriculum. Partnering with the community college has opened up many avenues of . . . ."

"Like I was saying," Miss Irene interrupted the principal before he broke into a full-on PowerPoint presentation. "They improved the suspension and switched to a small gas engine to increase . . . ." She looked at Big George and hesitated.

"The speed. Yes, dear. I'm quite aware of your need for speed," Big George said. "I may have done a little consulting work without your knowledge."

"As I said, we here at PGHS value our partnerships with community . . . ."

"I should have known Dretti would want your okay before they touched my . . . ."

"No, dear. Andy's questions were purely mechanical. He didn't ask my permission. You don't need it. I trust your good judgment."

"Ha!" Coach Frieh snorted. "Good judgment? Miss Irene?"

"Now, Coach," Big George said soothingly.

"No. He may have a point. *This time*," Miss Irene admitted. "After the classroom presentation, we went out to the track for the test run. I was coming down the straightaway in front of the home bleachers and had just reached top speed when the front end started to wobble."

"She was traveling at unsafe speeds on a public road!" Principal Dexter said to Officer Doug.

"Well, sir, I don't think they consider the high school track a public thoroughfare. And there isn't a posted speed limit that I'm aware of, is there?" the officer replied.

"Pffft. I was goin' fifteen, maybe sixteen miles an hour, tops. No matter how much I goosed her, I couldn't go any faster."

"That would be the restrictor plate. I didn't realize *you'd* be the test driver, dear," Big George said.

"I couldn't very well put one of the children at risk . . . or let them have all the fun." That explained the motorcycle leathers she was wearing and the helmet by her feet.

"But the unsafe driving!" Principal Dexter threw up his arms.

"That wobble made it a little more difficult to steer. I may have veered out of my lane."

"I was afraid she was gonna go off-roading, right through the end zone! And we still have three home games left," Coach said.

"Willful destruction of school property! Vandalism!" Principal Dexter pounded on his desk.

"I was worried about *her* safety, not the safety of the turf, sir.

13

Grass can be replaced. But there's only one Miss Irene. Thank goodness."

"But . . . but . . . she nearly ran me over! I was trying to redirect her, and she headed straight for me!" Principal Dexter's face was red from shouting, and I thought he may be developing an eye twitch.

"I was heading for the stack of high jump cushions at the end of the sprint lane. You kept getting in my way, you ninny! The kids had set up a crash zone there in case of an emergency."

"Miss Irene! What if you had . . . ." I got choked up just thinking about the *what if*.

"Oh, don't fret dear. As soon as I let off the throttle, that wobble cleared right up. Power dropped off, too. Next thing I knew, I was back to riding my 'slow-bility' scooter. Barely cleared four miles per hour."

"That would be the redundant safety feature the kids designed. You should be proud of them, Mr. Dexter. That's some top-level engineering," Big George said.

"Sounds like you were in the wrong place at the wrong time, Principal. Not sure it even qualifies as an accident report, seeing as how there was no actual harm done. 'Fraid there's nothing I can do here." Deputy Doug looked relieved as he headed for the door. "But let me know if she comes after you with that handicap card." Principal Dexter followed him out of the office, still sputtering and complaining.

Miss Irene grinned. "I may have been having a little fun with Dexter there at the end of the ride. Four miles an hour. Pfft."

"I wouldn't expect anything less from you, Irene," Big George said.

"Yep. There's your good judgment." Coach Frieh checked to

make sure the principal was out of earshot, then giggled in a very un-football-coach-like manner. "Should'a seen him! High steppin' like he was runnin' tire drills. That boy runs like Steven Seagal!"

Principal Dexter was waiting for us in the outer office as we filed through the door. His color had returned to normal, and he had straightened his tie, so I assumed he had regained his composure.

I was wrong.

"I have decided not to pursue charges against you at this time, Mrs. Truman, although I believe Deputy Doug is overlooking your wanton disregard for the principles we espouse here at Pleasant Glen High School. To wit, we expect our volunteers to model good behavior for our students, Mrs. Truman. I'm afraid your series of poor decisions this morning, culminating in the use of sexual innuendo in front of the children, leaves me no choice but to ban you from all future school events and school property."

"Oh, my!" Miss Irene stumbled backward as if he'd hit her. Big George caught her, wrapping his arms around her protectively. Miss Irene loved to be around young people She loved the hoopla of hometown ball games. She was already looking forward to all the Senior Night concerts and performances that would mark Trey's final year of high school. Dexter couldn't have hurt her more if he *had* hit her.

"Now see here, young man . . . ." Big George shook with anger.

"I got this, George," Coach Frieh said, stepping between the couple and Principal Dexter. "With all due respect, sir, I realize you are new to the community and your limited exposure to Miss Irene may have given you the wrong impression of her character. I'll admit, the woman is headstrong, annoying, insulting, and yes, sometimes a little vulgar . . . ."

"Is this supposed to be helping?" I asked. Coach held up a hand to quiet me, but finally got to the point.

"What you don't know, Principal Dexter, is that this woman raised six children of her own as a single mother and helped raise countless others – including me. She and Big George have helped even more through their internship program at Pleasant Glen Cycles and Motors and the scholarships they've provided. She was vice president of Pleasant Glen Savings and Loan at a time when some women didn't even have their own bank accounts. She's served her time on the school board and served up booster dogs in the concession stand. In short, sir, I can only hope to have a positive influence on half as many students as she has."

"Why Butch, you old softy," Miss Irene said, smiling at Coach. "I'm sorry I asked if that was a whistle in your pocket or if you were just happy to see me."

"Fine! Whatever! Just get out of my office before I . . . ." Principal Dexter balled up his hands and held his breath.

"*My* office," Miss Finestock said quietly, arching an eyebrow at his outburst. Principal Dexter exhaled loudly, then stomped to his office and slammed the door.

Miss Irene winked at Coach Frieh. "I should have asked if it was a starter's pistol."

"Crazy old bat," Coach muttered.

Miss Finestock took off her oversized glasses and rubbed her eyes. "He's not a bad principal. Just a little green. Sometimes the kids rub off on him." She nodded her head toward the commons area. It was filled with students, all with their heads down, thumbs flying across their phones. Someone had taped a "#FREEIRENE" sign to the office window, and I could see more on the walls of the commons.

"Don't worry, dear. I'll take care of things here." Miss Finestock's fingers danced across her computer keyboard. "We'll post a video on YouTube promoting the class' achievement, and I'll take down this one of Dexter's chicken dance. Eventually." She smiled and turned her monitor so we could see the clip of the principal running from a mobility scooter driven by an anonymous, helmeted driver. "It's gone viral!"

"As much as I enjoy watching your slow-speed chase, don't you and Julie have someplace to be?" Big George steered Miss Irene toward the door.

"Holy Moses! We're late! I'd better drive," Miss Irene said.

"But, I, uh . . . ." I looked at Big George, sure he'd see the fear in my eyes. He hadn't been exaggerating Miss Irene's "need for speed" earlier.

"Just try to keep it in low-earth orbit, dear," Big George said, before kissing her cheek. Then he turned to me and whispered, "Who do you think taught those kids about restrictor plates?"

Chapter 3

The morning's events seemed to have mellowed Miss Irene . . . a little. On the way to the airport, she drove a reasonable – for her – and consistent fifteen miles over the speed limit. She routinely used the mostly flat, straight, four-lane road as her own personal autobahn, so I figured any time I could actually read the road signs was a win. Her 1980s era Lincoln Town Car seemed to float down the highway like the land barge it was.

"I'm a lucky woman, Julie," Miss Irene said, watching the road ahead thoughtfully.

"Do you mean your scooter ride?" The thought of her hurtling down the track still gave me chills.

"Nah, I could handle that. I mean George." She glanced over at me and smiled. "After Frank, I wasn't sure I needed, or wanted, another man in my life. I had a few other beaus before George and I made it official. None of them seemed to stick. Maybe I was just too independent."

"How did you know Big George was the one?"

She shrugged. "It wasn't some big lightning bolt moment like in the movies, if that's what you mean. I think I was in love with George before I even knew I was attracted to him. We were busy getting the shop up and running and watching after the kids. I was riding The Scout on trips with the Motor Maids and George was making sure she was ready. One day, I realized he was always . . . there. And I knew I couldn't have done it without him. Or maybe that I didn't want to do it without him.

"After all these years, I still feel the same way. I can't imagine life without him." She shook her head. "No, that's not true. I *can*. But I'd rather not."

I thought about Joe, or more accurately, I thought about how much I missed Joe and how much I wished he was . . . here, more than he was. Or that I was there with him. Lately, our schedules had been so busy that we only managed to spend a day or two together, with a week or more between visits. Phone calls, texts and Skype were nice, but it was hard to build – or rebuild – a relationship with such limited contact.

Once we arrived at the airport, Miss Irene's mellow mood disappeared. She fussed and fretted over every little thing, despite the fact that we were plenty early. With her behind the wheel, we had made the hour-plus drive in less than forty-five minutes. I suggested we have a margarita in the airport bar, both to calm her nerves and to keep her from pestering the TSA agents any more than she already had, but she declined. I had never known her to pass up a margarita. Especially if I was buying.

"Beatrice is my 'glass is half broken' child," Miss Irene said. "If I'm not waiting for her at the gate, she'll think I've been kidnapped and have Homeland Security shut down the airport to look for me." I finally got her settled on a bench near the arrivals board and distracted her by asking about Beatrice.

"She's my oldest – nine months to the day after Frank and I married – and one of my 'old before their time' children. She's 70, goin' on 90. People have always asked us if we're sisters, poor dear.

"I don't know if it was first-child syndrome, or young and

inexperienced mother syndrome that made her this way. When she was a baby I worried about every little thing she did. By the time Henry – he's my tailender – came along, I had run out of worry. Of course, the twins – Francine and Jean, numbers four and five – may have had a lot to do with that. I swear those two shared one brain and some days neither one of them remembered to use it.

"Maybe Beatrice felt a responsibility to look after the younger ones. The divorce was hard on her. She was 10 when we split up and she thought Frank hung the moon. She likes George, and she knows Frank has his faults, but . . . . To tell you the truth, I was a little surprised she agreed to come back for the wedding. Although she's been to all of Frank's, so . . . ."

While Miss Irene was talking, Beatrice's plane arrived. We watched as passengers streamed into the greeting area. A frazzled-looking young woman carrying a backpack overflowing with stuffed animals staggered after two energetic little boys. Three middle-aged men wearing suits and carrying briefcases were studying their phones so intently they nearly collided. A young man in Army fatigues barely made it past the final checkpoint before a welcome party mobbed him.

As the crowd drifted toward the luggage pickup area, I noticed an elderly lady slowly making her way down the corridor. She was wearing a polyester pant suit that paired Pepto Bismol-pink slacks with a large-print, pink and white, short sleeve jacket. I wondered how her saucer-sized, rhinestone brooch ever made it through the security scan. A pink chiffon scarf, tied neatly under her chin, kept her white bouffant hair in place, while a chain of pink crystals secured her pink browline glasses.

"Mother!" she shouted, dropping her jumbo, lime-green tote

bag.

"Bumble Bea!" Miss Irene's face lit up. Then she turned to me. "Try not to gawp, dear. It's unseemly." The two women exchanged an awkward hug, briefly brushing cheeks before stepping an arms-length apart.

"And you must be Julie!" Beatrice clapped her hands with delight. "I've brought you a little surprise!"

One last passenger stood at the arrivals gate: Helen Westbrook. My soon-to-be ex-mother-in-law.

"Surprised?" Helen asked.

"Try not to gawp, Irene. It's unseemly," I muttered. I approached Helen, my arms out in a welcoming, but not quite hugging gesture. She took my hands in hers, squeezed them lightly, and smiled.

"I'm sorry for all the drama, dear," she said. "It was Beatrice's idea. Gary couldn't be here to meet me, and she just wouldn't hear of me getting a taxi. I hope you don't mind."

"Of course not! It's wonderful to see you!" I knew Helen was coming to Miss Irene's wedding – they were old friends – but I hadn't expected her to arrive so soon.

I helped the women gather their bags, then went to retrieve the car. Miss Irene and Beatrice settled into the backseat, catching up and going over plans for the week and the wedding. Helen joined me in the front.

"I have some business I need to take care of, so I decided to come back early," she said. "I don't want to intrude."

"Don't be ridiculous!" Beatrice said. "You're like family . . . er, um . . . ."

"We'll always be family, dear." Helen smiled at me, brushing away Beatrice's gaffe.

Helen had a gift for putting people at ease, while Beatrice seemed to have a gift for putting her foot in her mouth. That was just one of the differences between the two women. Although Helen was slightly older, she looked much younger. Helen's black slacks and cashmere sweater – worn casually draped over her shoulders – were timeless and tasteful and accentuated her lithe figure. I didn't think her two-inch pumps were practical for air travel, but I had never seen her wear any other type of shoe. I was fairly certain her feet had a permanent arch, like Barbie's.

I soon realized why Miss Irene had agreed to let me drive home.

"Hmmm. Going a bit fast, aren't we?" Beatrice stated more than asked.

I checked the speedometer. "No. Actually I'm right at the speed limit."

"Yes. Well. If God had wanted us to race through the Iowa countryside, he wouldn't have made Terry Branstad governor for life. Twice."

"Lighten up, Grumble Bea," Miss Irene said, patting Bea's knee. "If God hadn't wanted us to race through the Iowa countryside, he wouldn't have invented the V8 engine."

Beatrice's non sequitur had its desired effect. I eased up on the accelerator as I tried to follow her logic and set the cruise control to five under the limit. A steady stream of cars blew by us.

"I've missed autumn in Iowa," Helen said, providing a welcome change of topic. She was absentmindedly toying with her necklace – a single strand of gray pearls – as she took in the passing fields. The luster of the pearls matched that of her silver hair, which she wore in an elegant French twist, as always. "I've missed you, dear. And Emily. And Gary."

"I've missed you too, Helen." It was true. Helen had been a good friend to me even before she became my mother-in-law.

"I can't help but think that if I had been here all of this . . . unpleasantness could have been avoided."

"I don't think there was anything you could have done." That was true, too. I doubt Helen could have said anything to Gary to make him honor our wedding vows. And, since Gary had told me she had stood by his father despite his many affairs, I doubt there was anything she could have said to me that I would have wanted to hear.

"Perhaps," she shrugged. "But a little guidance, a little advice . . . the name of a good jeweler." She laughed as if she were joking, but I thought about her extensive collection of expensive jewelry and wondered how many of those pieces were "forgive me" gifts from Richard.

"I take it you're still living in Miss Irene's garage?" she asked.

"The apartment above her garage, yes." I smiled at her concern. Anything less than a big, sturdy house – preferably with a security system, and of course, her son – would not meet with her approval.

"A little . . . small, isn't it?"

"It's cozy. Perfect for one."

Helen nodded. "And your musician friend?"

"Joe lives out near Des Moines, on the family farm. He has a recording studio there. He travels a lot, so . . . ." Telling my husband's mother about my boyfriend was one of those awkward conversations I never expected to have. "We're taking things slow. I'm still figuring out who I am, I guess. What I want."

"Who you are? Darling, you're Julie Westbrook. You're Gary's wife and Emily's mother."

"That may have been enough . . . once," I almost said 'for you'. "But Emily's away at college, she doesn't need me . . . ."

"Emily still needs you. Your children always need you. In one way or another."

I knew she was right, but I also knew that I wanted more out of life. "And I'm building my event planning business," I continued.

Helen raised an eyebrow. "I'm sure you'll do wonderfully, dear. You've always had a talent for planning parties. But can you really turn that into a career? In Pleasant Glen? And why should you? Gary can take care of you, dear. I'm sure there will be plenty of parties to keep you busy with his new job. In fact, he is going to need you more than ever!"

"After Gary's . . . actions . . ." I still couldn't quite bring myself to say affairs, "I can't do it, Helen. We grew apart. We aren't in love anymore."

"Love isn't something you just fall in and out of. Love is something you decide. You find someone who needs you, someone who can take care of you, and you make it work. That's love. You two may not *like* each other very much right now, but that will change. Gary can take care of you, Julie. He wants to take care of you. And he needs you. Of course he loves you."

I knew arguing with Helen was pointless. Once upon a time I would have given in. Not now. I wanted to make her understand.

"Did you know Gary lied to me when Joe left all those years ago? Gary erased Joe's phone messages and threw away letters. He lied to Joe, too. Our entire marriage was based on lies." I still got angry when I thought about how Gary had manipulated us, and how easily I had fallen for it.

Helen stiffened. "I'm sure he had his reasons. He was looking out for you. What type of life could that musician have provided? You needed a family. A home."

That was, almost word for word, the argument Gary had made when I confronted him. An uncomfortable silence settled between us for the remainder of the drive. When we arrived at our . . . Gary's . . . house, Beatrice helped Helen with her luggage while Miss Irene and I waited in the car.

"Helen's right about one thing, dear," Miss Irene said. "Love is something you have to work at. Some people make it easier than others. And some make it damn near impossible."

Chapter 4

Miss Irene's bachelorette party began with dinner at Glen View Grille. I didn't exactly avoid Helen, but I didn't go out of my way to talk with her, either. That was easy enough to do. What started as a party of twelve – enough for a pickup game, Miss Irene pointed out – more than doubled in size. The Pleasant Glen grapevine turned a dinner with friends into an impromptu reunion of all PGHS girls basketball players.

A steady flow of diners stopped by to congratulate the bride-to-be – including Grant Cone, director of the Pleasant Glen Art Museum. Gary had told me that his mother and Grant had developed a special friendship before she moved to Florida. I noticed Helen blushed slightly when Grant greeted her, and she seemed distracted after he left.

When the ladies staged a spontaneous free throw shooting contest – really, what was management thinking leaving all those baskets of rolls sitting out? – we decided it was time to move on to The Bar and the band. Helen volunteered to help me return a couple of the older women to the nursing home before curfew. I was driving Miss Irene's Lincoln so, unfortunately, there was plenty of room. Besides, Helen's calming nature came in handy, as she charmed the orderly while the ladies smuggled in leftover desserts and alcohol. Miss Irene's friends may not have maintained her level of mobility, but they shared her zest for life.

"I'd like to apologize for my outburst this afternoon," Helen said, as we made our way downtown. "Your separation has been hard on me. I care deeply for you, Julie. I worry about Emily. She still needs both her parents. And Gary will always be my little boy."

"I know, Helen," I replied. Because I *did* know. I knew that no matter what her age, Emily would always be my little girl, and any slight to her would be a slight to me.

Helen gazed out the window pensively. "It was a lovely get-together. So many people I haven't seen in such a long time."

"Like Mr. Cone?" I knew I was being nosy and more than a little rude, but I couldn't help myself.

"Like Grant," she said, turning away from the window. "How much has Irene told you?"

I shook my head. "Gary told me you two were . . . close. He said Richard became jealous, and that's why you moved to Florida."

"Florida was *my* idea. After my affair with Grant – it was an affair, even though we were never physically intimate – I thought it best to leave. Grant is an honorable man. We were very fond of each other, and we had so much in common. I was an art major in college, you know." I knew Helen had an eye for decorating and that she was a Pleasant Glen College alumna – that's how we first met – but she never talked much about herself.

"Grant and I could discuss art for hours . . . or sit silently, sharing the experience. There's something about being in the presence of art that can be deeply emotional. These days people rush through an art gallery taking horrible pictures on their phones and miss all that. Why not just buy a book in the gift shop? Art is meant to be experienced and savored."

27

She paused, sighing deeply before continuing.

"Grant often invited me to accompany him to special events or notified me when pieces arrived for exhibit here. One night he called, terribly excited. There had been a mix up in a shipment. A piece was delivered that shouldn't have been. He wanted to share it with me before a special courier arrived for its return.

"Richard had just . . . started a relationship with another woman. He said this one was . . . different . . . special." She spat the words out. "He had . . . fallen in love with her. He thought we should . . . . I was vulnerable, Julie. Lonely. Empty." She dabbed a stray tear from her cheek. "Then Grant called. I thought perhaps we . . . . I just wanted to feel . . . wanted. Needed.

"I went to the gallery fully intending to . . . . I let myself in through the back door. A dim light spilled into the hallway from the conservation room. Grant had moved a small settee in from the lounge. He sat, staring at a canvas on an easel. A bottle of his favorite Cabernet and two glasses were on a table, forgotten. The look on his face was . . . beatific. He was completely absorbed in that painting. He didn't notice me standing in the doorway.

"Art . . . music . . . has the power to consume you. To transport you away from this world. I knew I could never compete with that. No woman could. The next day, I put our house on the market and told Richard we were moving to Florida."

"But, Richard . . . ."

"No. With Richard it was different. Richard's needs were physical. I knew he would tire of that woman the same as he had all the others. And I would be there for him when he did.

"Richard needs me, Julie. I organize the countless little things that make his life run smoothly, so that he can concentrate on his business. And I organize that, too. None of those other women could do that. He needs me. I'm *his* art. But I come at a price, like all fine art." A small, humorless smile flicked across her face. She touched the pearl necklace.

"He's a successful man, Julie. He's a successful man because of me. That makes *me* successful. You made Gary a successful man, but this promotion is not a done deal. He still needs you. Can you say the same for your musician?"

I shivered as Helen's words sank in. We had been sitting in the car outside The Bar while Helen finished her story.

"I forgot how cool September nights can be," she said. "The days are warm and beautiful, but once the sun goes down . . . . We should join the others. Miss Irene will be worried about you. And I think we could both use a drink."

Chapter 5

Six-on-Six had started their first set by the time Helen and I went inside. Miss Irene and her friends were at tables right in front of the stage. Bob had arranged the speakers so that the ladies would be able to talk without shouting and wouldn't have to remove their hearing aids.

The crowd was good-sized and mostly female. The PGHS football team and fans were on the road, another reason Bob agreed to host our party. Miss Irene's group had picked up some stragglers, including my frenemie Muffy – 1984, bench warmer – and her mother Shirley – 1965, starting guard. A few regulars poked around the edges, maintaining their home court advantage. That group included Melvin Steinhocker – 1953, head cheerleader – and his wife Norma – 1953, forward and focus of Melvin's cheers.

Many of the women wore PGHS "Phiting Pheasants" sweatshirts, although a few, Miss Irene included, had dug out their old "Galloping Glennies" apparel. This original school mascot, a crazed redhead wearing a tam-o'-shanter and kilt, had been dropped in the mid 1960s, more because of the kilt than cultural sensitivity. A particularly artsy member of the pep squad, influenced by a production of *Lysistrata* at the college, created an anatomically correct and generously exaggerated costume. After his halftime routine, everyone from the floor seats to the top of the bleachers knew what was – or wasn't –

under the Scotsman's kilt. Earlier mascots had only hinted at an answer.

I was still reading the room when Gary called to us from a nearby booth.

"Gary! What a surprise! I had no idea you'd be here tonight!" Helen's greeting was a little too enthusiastic, I thought, and seemed to catch Gary off guard.

"But you . . . I mean . . . ." he stammered as he stood to hug his mother. I couldn't see Helen's face, but I'd bet money she gave him "the look." He glanced up at me and smiled, recovering smoothly. "I mean, that was my plan, Mother. I got back to town a little earlier than expected. Surprise." After twenty-five years of marriage, I could tell when Gary was lying. I just didn't know why.

"Please, sit down," he said, ushering us toward his booth. "I'll get your drinks. Tanqueray and tonic?"

"Sapphire if they have it," Helen said.

"What would you like, Julie?"

"Um, yes. The same, please." Gary's question caught me off guard. I couldn't remember the last time he asked me what I wanted instead of just ordering for me. Between that and the lie, I was flustered. I stumbled as I stepped past him. He reached out to steady me, slipping his arm around my waist with more familiarity than I was comfortable with.

"It's good to see you, Julie. I've missed you." He flashed his deal-closing smile, complete with a dimple and sparkling blue eyes. Once upon a time that look would have melted my defenses and caused me to forgive him for forgetting my birthday – again – "working late" at the office – again – or whatever he had done to piss me off. Now it just made me . . . suspicious.

31

Bob edged between Gary and me, forcing us apart, and placed two drinks on the table. Then he practically pushed me into the booth and slid in right behind me. "I dusted off the Hendrick's, just for you, Helen. Saw you come in, figured you'd want the top of the top shelf. I hate to waste it on this one," he said, nodding at me.

Gary shrugged at Helen and remained standing.

"Julie might surprise you, Bob. And I'm flattered that you remembered my favorite drink . . . I think!" Helen had a delicate, lady-like laugh, but her face brightened, and her shoulders shook with delight.

"How could I forget? Thanks to you, this is all Liz will drink!"

"Oh, my! We had such fun on those trips up to the Dance-Mor, scouting bands for The Bar. Remember how we pestered you to book the Bandera Boys?" Gary looked as astonished as I felt by this little nugget of history. Helen was just full of surprises tonight. "I miss those days. How is your better half, Bob?"

"She's fine. Fine. Runnin' me ragged. She's in the kitchen, working on something for Miss Irene."

"Oh, Bob, I'd love to see her . . . ."

Bob shot me a worried look and hesitated before answering. "I . . . I'll go see if I can find her. She'd love to see you, too. I'll catch hell if she misses you. I'll . . . we'll be right back." Bob looked back at me again before getting out of the booth.

"You okay?" he asked me under his breath.

I smiled and nodded. I hoped I looked more confident than I felt.

As soon as Bob walked away, Gary moved to sit beside me. Before he could, Emily slid in and almost ended up with Gary on her lap. Helen's frown disappeared when she realized the intruder was her granddaughter.

"Gramma! I didn't know you'd be here!" Emily grabbed Helen's hands and leaned across the table to kiss her cheek.

"Well, I . . . but, you're not 21 yet, dear! You can't . . . ."

"I'm with the band! Had to bring in something from Chicago," she said, grinning.

I figured this was Joe's doing. I worried Emily was taking advantage of his connections to get backstage access, but Joe said he appreciated her perspective. It didn't hurt to have an attractive young girl around when negotiating with boy bands, either, he said.

"I'm not supposed to leave the back room, but I just had to come see you! And I have to be out by 10 o'clock when Chief Clancy's stopping by to check on Miss Irene, but that won't be a problem if you and Dad will take me out for pizza because I'm starving!"

I got the feeling Emily was up to something, too. The last time she talked that fast, we found out she had backed into the only other car in an otherwise empty parking lot.

"But . . . ." Helen hesitated. "Why don't we *all* go back to the house and catch up! The four of us can have a slumber party! I'll make pancakes in the morning."

"Eh, Bob needs Mom to keep an eye on Miss Irene," Emily said. She was out of the booth now, pulling on her grandmother's hand. "This will give us more time together. I just talked to Liz, and she's tied up but wants to meet you for lunch tomorrow. We can take Mom shopping after that! Please, Daddy?"

Neither Gary nor his mother could resist when Emily gave them puppy dog eyes. Helen eased out of the booth while Emily hugged me goodbye.

"I left a surprise for you in the back room," she whispered.

"Please tell me it's not dirty laundry."

"You'll see," Emily replied in a sing-song voice. She giggled excitedly and hurried to the door. Helen hadn't made it far before another old acquaintance stopped her.

I got out of the booth to join Miss Irene's group, but Gary stepped in front of me. He ran his hand down my arm, gently stopping me.

"I'm sorry about the . . . ambush, Julie. Mom's playing matchmaker. Or maybe it's re-matchmaker. She means well. She misses you. So do I. We're both worried about you."

I snorted. All this worry was starting to get on my nerves. "Poor, ignorant Julie, too stupid to take care of herself," I said.

"No, honey, it's not like that."

I had spoken more sharply than I intended. "I know. It's just . . . ."

"We remember how you were when he left the first time." Gary still refused to say Joe's name.

"Joe left because you lied to him!"

"He may have left because of me, but he could have returned at any time. He was gone for twenty-five years, Jules. I was here. I'm here now! Where is he?" I was tired of arguing. And I was afraid that Gary might have a point.

I *didn't* know where Joe was. We had talked briefly the night before, after his concert ended, but he hadn't replied to any of my texts since then. I knew he was busy, but this was unusual. Helen and Gary's double-barreled assault, coupled with Joe's absence, was undermining my confidence.

My phone rang. I could barely hear it over the crowd noise.

"That's probably him now," I said smugly. I pulled the phone

34

out of my purse and checked the screen.

"No, it's not." Gary sounded even more smug than I had. "'Shake It Off' is Emily's ringtone. She programmed it in my phone, too."

I looked up. Emily was standing by the door with her phone in her hand, waving at us.

"You don't know where he is, do you? Listen to me Jules. I've learned my lesson." Gary gently cupped my chin in his hand. "Give me another chance. Please."

He stood there looking like he had every intention of kissing me. My stomach gave a little flip, and I felt my face flush. Gary was good looking and charming. No wonder women were attracted to him. If I didn't know him so well, I would be too.

I gazed up into his eyes. "You are out of your freakin' mind if you think I want you back."

Gary laughed, tilting his head back and letting his eyes crinkle adorably. "Hmmm, someone's trying to quit swearing again."

He was handsome, charming, *and* he knew me well. I should have told him to fuck off. I should have told him I had a lot fewer things to swear about now that he was my soon-to-be ex-husband and I didn't have to worry about who else he was sleeping with. But of course, I didn't think of either of those clever comebacks until later. Instead, I stood there silently fuming, arms stiffly at my sides and hands balled into fists.

"Ah well, can't blame a guy for trying." Gary wrapped his arms around me in a bear hug that was both weirdly platonic and far too intimate for our current marital status. Or maybe it was just our current marital status that was weirdly platonic and too intimate. Before I could recover, he strutted off to join Emily.

Damn, he had a nice ass.

Emily's eyes darted back and forth between her father and me. She gave me a double thumbs up and a baffled look. I returned the thumbs up and hoped she hadn't noticed me checking out her dad's ass.

Bob was right. Hendrick's was wasted on me.

Chapter 6

The band launched into their last song of the evening, "Box Out," turning the entire room into a dance floor – or a basketball court. All the former basketball players assumed the boxing-out stance, crouching down with arms outstretched and butts pushed back. The rest of us tried to avoid getting booty bumped. I figured the local chiropractors would be busy the next few days.

I gathered the glasses from our table and took them to the bar, a habit from my old waitressing days. Bob had a fresh drink waiting for me.

"I thought you said Hendrick's was wasted on me," I said.

"It was. This is water. You're the designated driver, in case you forgot. And you're gonna want to be sober for the next part of the show. But I'm hoping to forget this." Bob nodded toward the dancers as he poured himself a generous glass of Templeton Rye.

After the cheers died down, the lead singer – the back of her jersey said her name was Wendy – stepped back up to the microphone. "We want to thank you for your support tonight. And we join you in wishing Miss Irene and Big George the happiest of marriages! You know, I used to be the center for the Keosaqua Quaking Quails, so I don't hafta look up to a lot of people . . . ." The crowd laughed at this because the girl couldn't have been more than five-foot-four from the base of her chunky Chuck Taylors to the top of her messy bun. "But I gotta tell you, those two are the real MVPs!" She paused again for the cheers.

"Since Bob's letting this game go into overtime . . . we're subbing in a couple blue chip players!"

Big George, wearing a powder blue, 1970s-style tuxedo, complete with ruffled shirt and cummerbund, walked onto the stage. "There's very little a man won't do for the woman he loves. That includes wearing this ridiculous monkey suit," he said.

"Take it off!" Miss Irene shouted.

"Don't you dare!" Bob yelled back.

Big George winked at Miss Irene. "Maybe later, dear. First, I'd like to sing a bit. I want to thank you ladies for taking such good care of my girl, but now it's time to say goodnight."

J.J. and Trey, wearing matching tuxes, joined Big George on stage and they began to sing in harmony.

Irene, goodnight

Irene, goodnight

I had heard Big George sing this many times as he left Miss Irene's. No matter how late he stayed at her house, he always returned to his house before dawn to make breakfast for J.J. and Trey. He wasn't fooling anyone with his early morning routine, but I thought it was sweet.

When Joe stayed with me, he would join in singing the last lines of the chorus, just like everyone in the crowd did now.

Goodnight, Irene

I tossed back what was left of my water like it was a shot of tequila, then stared morosely into the empty glass.

Goodnight, Irene

Deep in my sulk, I imagined I could hear Joe's voice cutting through the chaos.

I'll see you in my dreams.

A simple piano bridge played, sending a chill down my spine.

There was only one person who could coax that sweet sound out of Bob's old Steinway upright. I whipped around towards the stage. I hadn't imagined Joe's voice. Joe *was* here. Now. Singing the first verse, with a few fitting alterations.

Next Sunday night they'll be married

While I was pouting, I had missed seeing Joe sneak onstage – powder blue tux and all. He was sitting at the piano, looking out at the crowd and flashing that rock-star grin. It was all I could do not to rush the stage.

"Bob, you . . . it's . . . he's . . . ."

"You have no idea how hard it's been, keepin' this a secret," Bob said, beaming. "His flight to Chicago was delayed every which-way possible. Emily picked him up at O'Hare. And then Helen and Gary showed up! This is why I don't allow bachelor parties in here. Too stressful."

I made my way through the crowd and was waiting in the back hallway for Joe when he came offstage.

"Surprised?" he asked, sweeping me into his arms.

"Just a little. I was expecting a bag of dirty laundry!"

"Ahh, Emily. I think that girl has a future as a double agent. I saw Barry and his mom out front," Joe still wouldn't say Gary's name either, "but I couldn't do anything without spoiling things for Big George. Emily said she'd handle it."

"Oh, Joe! I've missed you so much. And today – with Helen and Gary – ugh." I rested my head against his chest. "I'm so glad you're here. That's all that matters."

Joe kissed the top of my head. "I'm afraid I have some bad news."

"Can't it wait, like, thirty seconds?"

"Whatever you say." Joe chuckled, a deep rumbling in his chest that vibrated through me. He tilted my chin up and kissed me.

"Hey, you two! I run a respectable place here. Move it along!" Bob called down the hallway. "Besides, Sophia's heading this way."

"Guess your thirty seconds is up. I don't have the energy to get into it with her right now. Or the time." He took my hand and led me toward the back door. "I don't suppose you parked out back, tonight?" I shook my head no. Joe hesitated and looked toward the crowd. We couldn't see Sophia, but her voice was getting louder. "We'd better take the long way around. It'll be just like running from the paparazzi!" He grabbed two backpacks as we passed the kitchen.

"Please tell me that's not dirty laundry," I said.

"That's waiting back at your apartment. Emily packed a few things for you."

"But why? Wait. What about Miss Irene? We can't just leave . . . ."

"Miss Irene and her posse are in good hands. I'll explain everything in the car." He led me out the back door, down the alley, and around to the front of the building. "Where's your sense of adventure? I'm trying to sweep you off your feet. I'm trying to be romantic. I'm trying to be dashing. I'm trying to . . . ." When we reached Miss Irene's car, he wrapped me in his arms again, and started kissing that spot on my neck just below my ear. He backed me up against the car and kissed me until I was breathless and wanting more.

"Ahem." Chief Clancy was standing by the front door of The Bar, watching us and tapping his finger against his watch. "If you're planning on making a quick getaway, then you'd better, you know. Get away."

"Trust me, Julie." After Gary's philandering, trust was something I had to work at. But Joe kissed me one last time, erasing any doubts I may have had. "Now drive, woman! Drive like Miss Irene!"

"I'm gonna pretend I didn't hear that," Chief Clancy said.

I carefully backed out of the parking space and only squealed the tires a little as I took the corner on a mostly yellow light. Joe told me to head for the highway on the edge of town and go north.

"Okay, this whole Bonnie and Clyde thing is intriguing," I said, "but when are you going to tell me what's going on?"

"I missed you, Julie. Being together but being apart thing is wearing me down. J.J. told me his dad wanted to do something special for Miss Irene, and I thought . . . well, those two obviously know something about keeping a romance alive. So, I rearranged a couple things and caught a flight back, and . . . here I am. For the night."

"For the . . . ."

"For a couple hours, actually. I booked us a hotel room up by the airport so we could spend as much time together as possible. It's not much, but . . . ."

"It's better than Skype. Thank you, Joe." I reached out to hold his hand. "So, how long exactly do we have?"

"I have to catch a shuttle at 4:30 in the morning."

"But it's . . . ." The dashboard clock said it was 10:45. I looked at Joe. Sadness darkened his hazel eyes. "It's better than Skype," I said again. "I guess I'd better drive like Miss Irene!"

I may have even shaved a couple minutes off Miss Irene's best time. Joe only coughed and grabbed the door handle a couple of times when I swerved around traffic. As we drove, he told me about all the delays he had faced on his emergency trip home, and I told him about Miss Irene's scooter escapade. During a lull in the conversation, I noticed his head begin to nod.

"Don't fall asleep on me now, Joe Davenport!"

"Not a chance!" He snapped to attention. "Especially not with the way you're driving."

"Hmph. You can criticize my driving after we get to the hotel."

"I had much more fun things in mind. And if this bench seat wasn't so wide, I'd give you a preview." Joe leaned over as far as his seat belt would allow, but still couldn't quite reach me.

"Oh no you don't! I can either drive or I can kiss, but I can't do both. Besides, by the time you slide all the way over here, we'll be at our exit."

Somehow, we managed to make it safely to the hotel. We even made it out of the parking lot, through the lobby and into the elevator without losing any of our clothes. Thank goodness our room was on the second floor. There's something about being in a small, enclosed space with Joe that . . . well, there's something about being in *any* space with Joe that makes it hard for me to keep my hands off him.

We made it into the room, stumbling blindly over the threshold, kissing and groping like a couple of teenagers parking on a dirt road. Our lust-fueled impatience made us as clumsy as inexperienced teens, too. I couldn't, for the life of me, figure out the combination of buttons and hook-and-bar closures that fastened Joe's rental pants. Joe wasn't doing much better at unhooking my bra. After yet another unsuccessful attack, he was ready to throw in the towel.

"This is great cardio, but it's getting us nowhere," he said, breathlessly. "Maybe we just need to slow down and change our tactics."

I reluctantly agreed. "Besides, I need to, you know, freshen up. I've been drinking water all night."

We slowly untangled our arms and legs. He sighed again as he backed away from me. "I'll be over here. On the bed. Waiting for you. And trying to get these ridiculous pants undone. What the hell does a cummerbund do, anyway?"

"I dunno. But, wow! Those polyester pants don't leave anything to the imagination. Or do you always keep a pair of socks in your pocket?"

"I'll let you find out for yourself," he said, smirking.

I tried to hurry, but by the time I came back out, Joe was sprawled on the bed, snoring softly. It was almost midnight. I kissed Joe's cheek and curled up beside him. He mumbled in his sleep and rolled over, putting his arms around me.

It was better than Skype.

Chapter 7

A ringing phone woke me from a deep, dreamless sleep. I could feel Joe's body next to mine – the gentle pressure of his arm around me, the warmth of his chest against my back. When I reached out to silence my phone, the pressure lifted, the warmth cooled. Joe had already gone.

It took me a minute to get my bearings. I was in a strange room – not my nightstand, not my curtains, definitely not my bedspread. I closed my eyes and stretched. There was a Joe-shaped hollow in the mattress next to me. His cologne lingered on the pillow. The events of last night came back to me in bits and pieces: the party, the drive, the hotel room.

Joe *had* been here.

He was gone now, but he had been here. He had flown half-way across the country to surprise me. To spend a couple of hours with me.

It was better than Skype. It was.

But now . . . all I felt was his absence. I knew Joe felt it too. What was it he had said? "Being together but being apart is wearing me down."

How much more could he take? How much more could *we* take?

My phone rang again. I rolled over and squinted at the nightstand, thinking it might be Joe calling. Just enough light filtered through the never-quite-completely-closed curtains to suggest it was still ridiculously early for anyone to be awake on a Saturday morning. Joe's flight had left hours ago, but because they were last-minute arrangements he wouldn't arrive in . . . Sacramento? Sarasota? Saratoga? . . . until late morning. He was most likely in an airplane or shuttling between flights. I hesitated, letting the call go to voicemail, before propping myself up on one elbow to look for my phone.

The hotel notepad was leaning against the alarm clock. Joe, knowing how blind I am first thing in the morning, had written I LOVE YOU in large block letters. What if I hadn't taken my contacts out last night? Would that thirty seconds have made the difference between sleeping with Joe and *sleeping* with Joe? There were some squiggles under the block letters. Emily had packed my contact case and solution but not my glasses. That was probably because they were . . . I wasn't sure where they were. I held the pad up to my nose and read the note.

Good morning, sunshine! I knew if I woke you, I'd never make the airport shuttle. That wouldn't be a bad thing, but the sooner I get this trip over, the sooner I can be back. Had to move yesterday's meeting to Tuesday. I should be back Wednesday. Have some things to do in Des Moines, but at least I'll be in Iowa −J

My phone rang again. Whoever was calling me was persistent, I'd give them that. Or they knew how hard it was to wake me in the morning. I reluctantly answered.

"Julie, it's Trey. Grandpa's in the hospital."

* * *

I threw my stuff in the backpack, grabbed Joe's rented tux, and called Emily from the elevator. Pleasant Glen being Pleasant

Glen, she already knew all about Big George. And then some.

Trey called me again when I was halfway home. They had moved Big George to a private room, and he was doing fine, but Trey was worried about Miss Irene. Trey was at the shop trying to restore some sense of normalcy and head off rumors.

By the time I arrived at the hospital, it was just after nine. Big George was sitting up in bed, flanked by J.J. and Miss Irene. A short-sleeved, navy blue work shirt with a Pleasant Glen Cycles and Motors logo covered Big George's standard hospital-issue, front-wrap gown. A scrap of faded aqua fabric – the only visible evidence of the gown – stuck out between two of the shirt buttons, dislodged by the EKG leads. The clear oxygen tube looped under his cheeks and over his ears. A red light glowed on the sensor covering his finger. Another tube snaked from his forearm to the IV pole. The flickering fluorescent lighting – only slightly more flattering than that in most dressing rooms – gave his skin a gray pallor.

Big George's eyelids fluttered, and his head nodded sleepily as they chatted. I had seen him dozing like this in his recliner at Miss Irene's many times. "Just resting my eyes" he always said. While I stood in the doorway watching, his eyes closed, his chin drooped to his chest, and his breathing slowed and grew heavy. Miss Irene and J.J. relaxed, sinking back in their chairs. They dropped their masks of cheer and let their faces sag. The tears that had been welling up in Miss Irene's eyes slowly dripped down her cheeks. Worry lines creased J.J.'s face.

I sat in the chair next to Miss Irene, took her hand in mine and gave it a squeeze. She smiled weakly and sniffed.

"He's doing good, Julie, really he is." She glanced at J.J. then laughed softly. "I know *we* don't look like it, but George is okay . . . ." Miss Irene shook her head, sniffed again, and turned to watch Big George.

"They've ruled out a heart attack, so they're running more tests, taking more blood, asking more questions. Dad suggested it was, and I quote, 'that damn cummerbund'." J.J.'s impression of his dad made even Miss Irene chuckle.

Big George grumbled in his sleep, which Miss Irene interpreted for him as "Watch your manners, son."

J. J. rubbed his hands over his face, then leaned forward, resting his elbows on his knees. "Not knowing what we're up against is the hardest part."

A pretty nurse, her blonde hair pulled back in a low ponytail, slipped silently into the room. As she passed by J. J., she ran a hand across his shoulder and gave him a reassuring pat and a warm smile. "He's gonna be fine honey. Don't you worry." She crossed to Big George's bed, checked the monitors and repositioned the clip on his finger.

Big George's eyelids fluttered. "*Angels 'n Ariels . . .*" he said, slurring his words.

"Now Mr. Monroe, I told you my name is Arianna, and I'm afraid I'm no angel." She gently adjusted the oxygen line and smoothed his white hair back into place.

"Ahh, poetic license m' dear. For my angel, Red Molly, over there." He nodded at Miss Irene. "*Gray hair 'n . . . leather . . . .*"

His voice quavered as he half-sang the words. His eyes shut again.

Miss Irene hiccupped as she tried to hold back tears.

"He's gonna be drowsy for a while. It's the drugs. He seems to be a bit of a lightweight with the painkillers," the nurse said. "I understand he doesn't take medication . . . of any kind?" She gave

Miss Irene a questioning look. "*Any*? At all? At his age?"

"No, never has." Miss Irene sighed, watching Big George sleep. "Never needed any."

"That's . . . impressive. You're a lucky. I mean, he's . . . well. It's just . . . ." She looked at J.J. and bit her bottom lip. "Huh." She started to leave but stopped at J.J.'s side. "My name's Ariel . . . I mean Arianna. I'll be here all morning if you need anything. *Anything*." She walked to the door, then looked back over her shoulder at J.J., one hand on her hip. "Call me."

"Friend of yours?" I asked, after she left.

J.J. angrily crossed his arms over his chest. "Never met her before," he said brusquely, looking at the floor. Miss Irene snickered.

"Dad had all the symptoms of a heart attack. Or of an adverse reaction to . . . erectile dysfunction medication," J.J. grumbled.

"I told the doctors Big George never had any problems in *that* department," Miss Irene said, chuckling some more.

"And they all remembered Miss Irene's little pole-dancing escapade," J.J. added, looking disgusted.

"So the nurses are hoping that his . . . ability runs in the family. J.J.'s become very popular."

"Can't even get a cuppa' coffee in the cafeteria without someone slipping me their phone number. And I could really use some."

"Why don't you take Julie with you. She could run interference. Or crowd control."

Our giggles must have disturbed Big George, because he snorted and stirred. He opened his eyes and looked around warily until he spotted Miss Irene. He smiled and stretched out his hand to her. She leaned forward and took his hand, holding it with both of hers.

"I love you, dear," she said.

Big George smiled and nodded. His eyelids fluttered again, and he sang softly, *"If fate should . . . give you my Vincent . . . ."*

Then he fell asleep again. Miss Irene choked back a sob.

"I can't do this. I can't do this anymore. I won't let you do this, George. I won't!" She dropped his hand and scurried from the room. I started after her, but J.J. stopped me.

"Let her go, Julie. She needs a little time. She's been holding it in since we got here. She wouldn't let Trey see how upset she was. She won't cry in front of Dad. Give her some time."

"But what was Big George talking about? Arianna said it was the drugs, but he wasn't just rambling."

"No, it's a song. 'Vincent Black Lightning.' A love song, I guess. About a guy and a girl and . . . well, a Vincent Black Lightning."

"A *what*?"

"It's a motorcycle. A rare, vintage motorcycle. Fastest production bike for its time. It's like Joe's bike . . . on steroids."

I was just about to screech *Joe's what?* when the rational part of my brain took control of my mouth and shoved my insecurities back into the dark, little cave they crawled out of. This was not the time or place to fuss about a motorcycle, not even a *secret* motorcycle.

I'm not sure why the idea of Joe not telling me he had a motorcycle bothered me so much. I mean, it's not like I had found out he had a wife or child, or an outstanding warrant. Maybe it reminded me too much of Gary and all his secrets. But Joe was *definitely* not Gary. If Joe didn't want to tell me he had a secret, super cool motorcycle, I'm sure there was a good reason for it. Probably.

Maybe.

I hoped.

Chapter 8

As the sedatives and pain meds wore off, Big George's condition improved – although the extra attention did make him uncharacteristically cranky. By late-afternoon, it was all Miss Irene could do to convince him to stay overnight for observation like Doc Houseman suggested. Big George gave in only when the nurses agreed to move a bed in for Miss Irene.

"Not that we'll need it," he said. That ornery twinkle was back in his eye.

"Just remember Dad, they're tracking your vitals at the nurses' station. If your heart rate goes up, you could draw a crowd," J.J. said.

"And *you'll* get more phone numbers." Big George's sense of humor had returned as well.

Doc Houseman agreed that if Big George – and Miss Irene – behaved and his vital signs stayed strong, Big George could go home with Miss Irene the next day. None of us really believed he would be staying in her first-floor guest room, but it did give him an excuse not to make the predawn trip back to his house.

"Usually I tell folks to quit smoking, watch their cholesterol and get more exercise," Doc said. "But you're in better shape than I am . . . and nearly twice my age. Whatever you're doing, keep doing it. I'd tell you to avoid stress, but with Gypsy Rose Lee here . . . ."

"There's never a dull moment with her around. And I

wouldn't have it any other way. She keeps me young, Doc. She keeps me alive." Miss Irene, who had been studying the monitors and not the conversation, flinched when Big George patted her hand. She responded with a weak smile and a vague "mm-hmm," then turned her attention back to the monitors.

With Big George on the mend and overnight accommodations secured, J.J. and I were both sent home for the night. I called Emily with an update and let her and Helen convince me to join them for dinner.

"You shouldn't be alone, Julie," Helen said. "I know how upset you are about Big George. You need to be with family." I hated to admit that she was right. Even though Big George's episode seemed to be an isolated and unexplainable event, it was a harsh reminder that he and Miss Irene were not as young as they acted.

I wanted to call Joe. I wanted to be *with* Joe. I wanted to feel his arms around me, to hear him tell me everything was going to be alright. I wanted to tell him how much I loved him and missed him, and to hear him say the same.

But I didn't.

I knew he was getting ready for a show and didn't need to be distracted – not that he would tell me that. Well, I mean he might tell me I was a distraction, but he would say it in his low, rumbly, sexy voice that made my legs turn to jelly. And he would follow that up with a very detailed description of what I could do to distract him and all the ways he could distract me. We really needed more than ten minutes alone together while we were both awake and able to distract each other without crashing a car.

I settled for sending him a brief text, not mentioning anything about Big George or the Vincent. I told him I'd been thinking of him and that I needed to take a cold shower. Then I actually *did* take a cold shower, which only proved to me that nothing short of a polar plunge could cool my desire for Joe. And with my luck, I'd probably have a hot flash mid-plunge that would melt the icecaps and contribute to global warming.

* * *

After the drama of the last day and a half, I was looking forward to a quiet, *ordinary* evening with family – even if an evening with almost ex-family members wasn't very ordinary. We certainly didn't have to run from the paparazzi, but I wouldn't say that the evening was dull, by any means.

Gary answered the door in jeans and a black Polo-brand polo that were both slightly faded and form fitting. His damp hair was a little longer than usual and curled slightly at the nape of his neck. This was a new look for him. It was casual and relaxed. And sexy.

It also made me feel guilty. I had always scheduled Gary's haircuts. Just like I had always taken care of the laundry – whether it was adding a little vinegar to the rinse for darks or taking homemade cinnamon rolls to the dry cleaner who, coincidentally, always made sure Gary's shirts had just the right amount of starch.

Helen was right. Gary was the type of man who needed a little female guidance to reach his full potential. For years, I had provided that guidance. Gary had needed me. Joe took care of those details for himself. I kind of missed being needed.

Without thinking, I reached up to brush Gary's hair off his collar. He grinned, displaying his dimple. "I know, I know. Mom's already told me to get it cut. I've just been too busy to find a new barber out in Des Moines." He glanced toward the kitchen and lowered his voice. "Besides, it's driving Mom nuts, so that's kinda fun."

"It looks good on you," I said. And it did. Not only was he good looking and charming, he had a good sense of humor. And he smelled good – he had a clean, fresh from the *hot* shower smell that clung to him tighter than his polo clung to his biceps. It was an irresistible combination, and I was sure he wouldn't have any trouble gaining the love and attention of a good woman . . . or one like Sophia. I couldn't decide whether bringing those two together would solve all my problems or result in a new problem of epic proportions. Either way, the thought of the two of them together was a welcome distraction whenever Helen dropped a subtle or, more likely, not-so-subtle hint about Gary and I reconciling. Well, that and multiple glasses of wine. Gary seemed embarrassed by his mother's behavior, which I found even more charming. All things considered, it was a very pleasant evening.

The evening was *so* pleasant that I agreed to go to Mass the next morning as a family. This was the most time Gary and I had spent together since . . . I couldn't remember when.

Gary is a devout Mother Christ-Er, nodding off religiously at St. Cunegundes' each Mother's Day, Christmas and Easter. Father Martin was so surprised by Gary's unexpected appearance, that Mass was delayed while he checked the calendar. Apparently inspired by the return of a number of lost sheep, Father launched into a spirited homily that caused a lot of squirming in the pews.

Yea, verily, the congregation of St. Cunegundes' weathered the fire and brimstone mightily, and their blessings were bountiful.

The faithful left Mass inspired and confident in their role as the chosen ones. Thus restored to their rightful place at the head of the Pleasant Glen gossip grapevine, they were eager to share the good news at the post-service, inter-faith brunch buffets.

That morning the St. Cunie's flock had witnessed the return of the prodigal son Gary and his blessed mother Helen, as well as the visitation of holy Beatrice. The Lazarus-like recovery of Big George – a de facto Catholic – was matter-of-factly attributed to the ceaseless prayers and tithing of Miss Irene. But lo, the blessing cup overfloweth-ed when the congregation discovered in their midst my best friend and recent divorcee, the jezebel Vanessa, accompanied by a handsome male stranger.

Vanessa's reputation at St. Cunie's had been tarnished when she – distraught that her husband had left her for another man – slept with Gary, my then-current husband. Gary – distraught that I might leave him because I found out he was having an affair with a co-worker – had slept with Vanessa in an effort to destroy our friendship and cut off my only means of escape . . . and because, as he said, "Van's pretty hot when she cries."

I had forgiven Vanessa, more or less, but many of the St. Cunie's flock were not as understanding. Her past transgressions were momentarily forgotten when the Altar and Rosary Society members met her charming guest – who bore a striking resemblance to a young Lee Majors as Heath Barkley in *The Big Valley*. With redemption so close at hand, Vanessa wisely chose not to reveal that Steve Austen was her ex-husband's new spouse, or as she called him, "my ex-husband-in-law."

"They'll find out soon enough," she said. "Mom and Dad want to host a belated wedding reception for Michael and Steve. And Steve wants you to plan it."

After feeding more fuel to the rumor mill fire by attending brunch *en famille* – a brunch at which Gary paid more attention to me than to the twenty-something waitress – Emily and her clean laundry returned to college, and I made plans for a much needed, relaxing motorcycle ride.

The Scout had other ideas.

Despite her age, Big George's mechanical magic kept The Scout running like new. He had done everything possible, short of changing out her original systems, to make her comfortable and easy for Miss Irene – and now me – to ride. Miss Irene had bought The Scout in 1955, hoping to cure her husband Frank's restlessness. Big George had shined her up, and then Frank had taken a shine to George's wife, Doris.

Granted, The Scout could be a little temperamental. Usually a few sweet nothings whispered to her carburetor were all it took to put her in the mood. That day she was downright mulish. I pleaded. I caressed the curves of her gas tank. I may have promised her a hot wax and pedicure, noticing her glossy black paint was dull and her white fender skirts seemed dingy. Finally I leaned forward in the saddle and, resting my head on top of her gas tank, told her I was worried about Big George too.

"But he's fine. The doctor said so. There's nothing to worry about. He's fine. We'll all be fine."

I hugged her and kissed the top of her horn, checked the choke setting again and rose out of the seat to kick start her. She gave a couple half-hearted coughs, then started with a stuttering cadence. We sat in the driveway while I let her warm up, adjusting and readjusting the timing advance. When the sound of her engine finally kept a steady tempo, we set off into the warmth of the mid-September afternoon.

It was a beautiful day. The tree tops were starting to show the first colors of fall. We rolled past green and gold pin-striped corn fields and plush carpets of emerald soybeans speckled with yellow. But something was off. The Scout felt sluggish pulling away from stop signs and climbing the rolling hills. I breathed a sigh of relief as we coasted into valleys and shaded curves. When we pulled out to pass a tractor, I worried we might not make it, something I'd never had to consider before.

Big George must have felt a disturbance in The Force. He came out to meet us as soon as I pulled into Miss Irene's driveway.

"Scout giving you troubles, dear?" he asked.

"Eh. She's . . . ." I knew better than to outright lie to Big George. "I couldn't get the timing advance right, I guess."

"Hmm, I thought I had that worked out. I'll wipe her down and take a look."

"Julie can do that," Miss Irene said. She had followed Big George through the back yard, although at a much slower pace than usual. She pulled her cardigan closer and shivered. I was wearing a light, mesh riding jacket and started to sweat now that I wasn't in motion. "Julie can clean The Scout up and put her away. You need to come inside before you catch a chill." I detected a distinct shuffle to her step and a stoop to her posture as she headed back to the house.

"Yes, dear. Right behind you," he said without much enthusiasm. "Neither of us slept well last night. A hospital must be the worst place to rest. About the time one of us would nod off, a nurse would come in to see how we were doing." He shook his head and patted The Scout's headlight affectionately. "Bring her by the shop in the morning. I'll take a look at her."

Big George stepped toward the house, then looked back at me.

"I'm worried about her, Julie."

Chapter 9

Monday morning I coaxed The Scout to life, and we limped to the shop. I took a couple laps around town, trying to get The Scout's motor warmed up and hoping to work out whatever kinks were holding her back. Keeping her upright while we crawled away from stop signs made me nervous, so I drove the back route through quiet neighborhoods where I could just "slow and go," instead of coming to a complete stop.

Pleasant Glen Cycles and Motors is located one block south of the historic town square in a squat, red brick building originally built as an auto dealership in 1910. The huge windows that once displayed Ford Model T's and Iowa's own Colby automobiles were now filled with a mix of vintage and new motorcycles of many brands.

I drove around to the alley and pulled up to the service bay doors. Alex, the top mechanic – after Big George – walked me past Big George's usual work station. The boss was waiting for me in J.J.'s office, he said. "Papa Bear is a little growly this morning. But please don't tell him I said that. I like working here."

Big George was sitting behind J.J.'s desk with the chair tipped back and his feet propped up on a partially opened desk drawer. His eyes were closed, his chin rested on his chest, and his hands were folded across his stomach. It reminded me of how he had looked dozing in the hospital bed, and I wondered if he should be at work.

"Just resting my eyes, dear. Come in and sit down," he said, without opening his eyes or moving. "They're trying to kill me, Julie-girl."

"Who is?" I sat across from the desk on the couch J.J. had fashioned from the backseat of an old Thunderbird.

"Miss Irene and J.J."

"Don't you think you're being a little overly dramatic, Dad?" J.J. rolled his eyes at me as he walked into the office. He was carrying a to-go tray with three large cups of coffee.

"Watch your manners, son." Big George cautioned, still not opening his eyes. "How are the girls at the bakery?" He finally opened one eye to watch for J.J.'s response.

"Fine." J.J. removed the cups from the carrier, almost slamming them down on the desk top. "Velma sends her regards. As do the rest of them."

Big George snorted and sat up. "I bet they do." He examined one of the cups. "And to which lovely lass does this phone number belong?" He turned it around so that I could see the writing.

"Maybe it's Tiffany's," I said, studying the signature on another cup. "I've always wondered – when they dot the 'i' with a little heart, does that change the pronunciation?"

J.J. glared at me, picked up the final cup and read it. "Fer' the love of . . ." he muttered while emptying the cup into his travel mug.

"I think they spelled your name wrong there, son," Big George said nodding at the cup. Someone – perhaps Tiffany-with-a-heart – had written "Stud Muffin" on it.

"No, Dad," J.J. sighed. "That was for you. From Velma. She told me I was too young for her, but offered to introduce me to her niece. *That* did not sit well with Tiffany."

J.J.'s face was tuning an angry purple, so I decided to change the topic before he *did* try to kill someone.

"Why did you say Miss Irene was trying to kill you, Big George?"

"When we got home from the hospital yesterday, Irene insisted I rest – apparently she thought the five-minute car ride had worn me out. Then she insisted I rest while she 'prepared my room for me,' followed by more resting while she made dinner. Any time I got up out of the recliner, she fussed and squawked so much I thought *she* would have a heart attack."

"She's just a little worried, Dad," J.J. said quietly.

Big George sighed. "I know son, but I'm not some fragile doohickey you put under glass. Doc gave me the all-clear . . . ."

"Doc said you should take it easy . . . ."

"Doc *said* I'm in better shape than he is." Big George rested his elbows on the desk, leaned over and frowned at J.J.

"Okay, so Miss Irene may have gone overboard with the resting," I said. Big George sat back in his chair and turned his frown on me.

"That was just the start, Julie-girl. While I was 'resting' she baked all the moisture out of the chicken and paired it with creamed spinach and lime jello. Never thought I'd miss hospital food.

"As soon as we finished dinner, she announced it was time for bed. And it was only 6:30, for heaven's sake! Most nights I would have thought she had something special in mind . . . ." J.J. coughed, but Big George let it slide. "Turned out she really did put me in the downstairs guest room! But with Beatrice upstairs in her old room, I figured it was for the sake of appearances." J.J.

covered his face with his hands. "So, I went to bed and waited. When Irene finally came in, she was wearing a long flannel nightgown. I told her I had been hoping for the naughty nurse outfit...."

"Dad!"

"... but I could play the Big Bad Wolf instead."

"DAD!"

"She burst into tears and ran – well, shuffled quickly – up the stairs, sobbing all the way. She slammed her bedroom door in my face. And locked it."

"Oh, George," I said sympathetically.

"I tried to talk to her. I begged her to open the door. I told her I was sorry I upset her, even though I wasn't sure what I had done. She cried harder." Big George slumped in his chair and picked at the lid of his coffee cup.

"After a bit, I heard a sniffling from behind me. Beatrice had stuck her head out her door and was standing there, eyes big as silver dollars. She had the same worried look she used to get as a child when there was a thunderstorm brewing. 'Is Momma alright?' she asked me, her voice all quiet and scared. Poor little Bumble Bea," George shook his head. "She always did worry about every little thing. I told her Irene would be fine, that she was just a little tired. I said we all needed a good night's sleep, and that everything would be better in the morning. 'Course it wasn't.

"Irene had the heat turned up so high I thought I'd roast – even with the window open. I was in a froth all night, tossing and turning, worse than in the hospital. This morning she served me lumpy oatmeal with tinned peaches. And tea. Tea for heaven's sake! Then I get to the shop and J.J.'s coffee looks like something he cleaned out of a carburetor. Tastes like it too!"

"Hey! It's shop coffee! It's supposed to be sludge! Keeps the customers from gettin' too cozy. Besides, I went to the bakery for you. Talk about your froths! I was lucky to get out of there alive!"

"Musta' been some froth for you to forget my donuts," Big George grumbled.

J.J. shuddered. "If you'd seen the lascivious way Tiffany handled the baked goods you'd understand."

"But why?" I asked. Big George was shaking with silent laughter.

"Why? *Why?* Why did a woman I barely know try to proposition me with a pastry?" J.J.'s face went straight to purple this time. "You saw 'Nurse Friendly' at the hospital. The lack of . . . performance-enhancing drugs . . . in Stud Muffin's history is the hottest news to hit the pavement in Pleasant Glen in years! The women in this town have lost their minds. My refrigerator is overflowing with casseroles. Trey's girlfriend's dad made her break up with him and Trey's phone has been ringing nonstop since she did. I've had to put my cell phone on silent and bring one of the boys out from the shop to answer the office phone and deal with walk-ins."

"Most men would be happy to be Pleasant Glen's most eligible bachelor," Big George said, smirking.

"I'm not most men! I have a business to run, a son to raise. A father to keep out of trouble. I don't have time for this foolishness!"

This was quickly becoming one of those conversations you don't want to be a witness to, but you can't tear yourself away from.

Big George studied J.J. for a moment, then spoke to him gently.

"Junior. It's been sixteen years since Allison passed away. She was a wonderful woman, but she wouldn't want you to mourn her forever." J.J. hung his head. I had never heard him talk about Trey's mother, although I had seen pictures of her at their house. "You need someone, son. Trey will be going to college soon. I'll be gone . . . ."

J.J.'s head snapped up. "Dad! Don't talk that way!"

"No, no. I mean I'll be moving in with Irene. You'll be rattling around in that house by yourself. But now that you mention it, I *am* 90 years old. I do have an expiration date – we all do. And none of us knows when that might be. You need to get out there and enjoy life, son. Follow up on a few of those phone numbers."

Just when things were getting good, my phone rang. I quietly excused myself and went out into the showroom to answer it.

"Hey, um, Jules . . . hang on a sec." It was Vanessa. More or less. The connection was sketchy, and there was a lot of road noise and honking in the background. She paused, and I heard the muffled scritching sound made by a cell phone being placed against a shoulder – the old-fashioned 'mute' button.

"Go around. Go AROUND, you asshat. No, not you, Steve. Yes, of course, you'd be more of an ass-fedora. Hang back a bit, don't crowd her." Steve's reply was garbled. *"I know he flipped you off, but he had a gun rack in the back window. Let it go. Let HIM go. You're gonna have to take one for the team, bud."* More garbling from Steve. *"No. I will not play 'I Can't Drive 55' again . . . No 'Highway to Hell' either."*

"Okay, Jules, you still there? Good. Have you seen Miss Irene this morning? Or her car?"

"No. I'm down at the shop. She and Beatrice had talked about visiting Frank today. They must have left before I did."

"Well, the thing is . . . . *Slow down, hon. Slower. Slowwwww-er. WATCH IT STEVE!*" I heard a faint smack. "*Sorry 'bout that. Mom-belt. Reflex. No. You won't have a bruise. Pussy.*" Despite not having children of her own – or maybe because of that – Vanessa tended to throw her arm out a little more violently than necessary to restrain fellow passengers whenever the car slowed quickly. Neither of our mothers had ever fully trusted seat belts, and we both had picked up on that habit. "*How the heck can she slow down anymore and still keep that land barge rolling?*"

"Van? Van, are you okay? What's going on?"

"Steve and I are heading up to River City. He heard there was a soft-opening for that trendy new hair salon today, so we . . . ." That hurt. Vanessa and I had made plans to go to the grand opening *together* next week. I was glad she and her ex-husband's new husband were getting along so well, but I was a little jealous, too. ". . . Anyway, traffic was all snarled up just past Crawfordsburg and when we finally got to the front of the pack, well, it looks like Miss Irene's Lincoln, but they're only going like, forty-five . . . ."

"*THIRTY-FIVE!*" This time I could hear Steve loud and clear.

"Check that, *thirty*-five, and I know Miss Irene drives a little faster than that. So, we passed them . . . ." Vanessa was interrupted by Steve, who mumbled excitedly. "Yes Steve, we passed *very* carefully because they were taking up more than their share of the middle of the road. Steve has a new Prius, and he's a little . . . protective. *Any*way, all I could see was a little tuft of white hair over the steering wheel. So we pulled off and waited for them to catch up and then pulled in behind them and now we have our hazard lights on and we're kind of the unofficial escort. I didn't want to call the cops until I checked with you, but Jules, I don't think I can take this much longer. All the honking and the weaving and . . ." Vanessa switched to a semi-whisper, *"Steve is driving me fucking nuts."*

"WHAT?" Steve shouted. Vanessa's cell-phone whisper, much like her drunk-whisper, is not very whispery.

"Not that I blame you, honey, but you need to Calm. The Fuck. Down. What should we do, Jules?"

Normally, I would have run this by Big George, but given his condition and how worried he already was about Miss Irene, I didn't want to add to his stress. I couldn't run it by J.J., because he is completely unable to keep a secret from his dad. It must be a family trait, because Trey can't keep a secret from J.J, so telling him was only a slightly less direct hotline to Big George. And Joe was far, far away and probably in the middle of a rehearsal.

I was on my own. Suddenly being a strong, independent woman wasn't quite so fun.

"Big George said Miss Irene has been acting strange . . ." Vanessa interrupted me with a snort, and I conceded, adding "-er than usual. I'll run by the house just to make sure she didn't loan her car out." Vanessa snorted again. I knew as well as she did that Miss Irene never let anyone besides Big George or me drive that behemoth. Not that anyone would want to. "I have a bad feeling about this. If you guys can follow her a little longer, I'll try to catch up with you . . . ."

"Catching up isn't going to be a problem, Jules." I heard Steve laugh. "What are you going to do after that? *No, Steve, a grenade launcher is not an option. You have no idea how bad her aim is."*

I sighed. Steve had read my mind and Vanessa had a point.

"One crisis at a time, Vanessa. I have no idea what's going on. Please, just keep an eye on her."

I speed-walked the most direct route home, thanking the fashion gods who made yoga pants an accepted staple of casual wear and cursing myself for not wearing my Fitbit that morning. As I feared, neither Miss Irene nor her Lincoln were there. I hopped in my Mini-Cooper and was heading north when Vanessa called to let me know they had followed Miss Irene – at great peril – to The MidWay Diner, mid-way between Pleasant Glen and River City. While Steve ranted in the background, Vanessa told me how Miss Irene had exited the highway, blew through a stop sign and pulled into the parking lot, all while maintaining her 35-mile per hour speed. Vanessa promised they would try to keep her at the restaurant until I could get there.

Chapter 10

I made the thirty-minute drive to The MidWay in twenty minutes, which was still five minutes slower than Miss Irene's record time. That day, however, it took her almost an hour to make the same drive. Mathematical story problems like this are why I majored in English. Regardless of which formula you used to solve for X, I was able to join the quartet before they finished their first cups of coffee.

Steve and Vanessa sat together on one side of the booth, flicking a packet of sugar between them. Miss Irene absentmindedly stirred her drink, clinking the spoon against the sides of the cup. Beatrice sat next to her, staring out the window.

Miss Irene and Beatrice were wearing matching floral outfits that looked, even to my un-fashion trained eye, like the bastard child of a muumuu and a house dress left unattended in a dark closet for too long. Despite the mid-September warmth, they had dark cardigans draped over their shoulders. Their white hair was spun into matching clouds, and identical, crystal-beaded chains tethered their glasses. Miss Irene was usually a sharp dresser, but now she looked like an unpaid extra from "The Golden Girls." I wondered how far Beatrice's influence extended beyond her mother's questionable clothing choices.

I pulled a chair over and signaled to the waitress for another round.

"So! Isn't this a pleasant surprise!" I said with forced cheerfulness. They all blinked at me, slowly coming out of their self-induced trances. I took advantage of their momentary distraction to grab both the sweetener and the spoon.

"Surprise? But you said she . . . ." Steve turned to Vanessa, a look of confusion on his face.

"Yes! Surprise!" Vanessa nodded her head toward Miss Irene and Beatrice. "What a totally random coincidence, running into them here. By chance." Steve was not yet accustomed to our Lucy and Ethel-style cues and harebrained schemes.

"But when we were stuck behind them on the highway, you said . . . OW!" Steve winced. I guessed, based on personal experience, that Vanessa had kicked him in the shin to "gently" suggest he stop talking. "What was that . . . ." Steve winced again. I also knew from experience that Vanessa wouldn't stop kicking until he stopped talking. Vanessa made a quick "zip your lips" motion.

"Oh . . . right. Surprise." Steve was a fairly quick learner.

"I forgot how bad the traffic is on this road," Beatrice said. "All those cars racing by us! And the honking! I had to ask Mom to pull over. My nerves were shot."

We sat quietly while the waitress poured our coffee. Beatrice slid her cup past her mother for a refill, but Miss Irene shot her hand out to cover it before the waitress could pour.

"We'll have more hot water, please," Miss Irene said.

The waitress put a hand on her hip and chewed her gum noisily. "You need a tea bag this time, or are you O.K.?" she asked.

"We're fine," Miss Irene answered. "We brought our own. Special blend." I looked at the tag hanging out of the tea pot. I could clearly read "Lipton."

Beatrice slumped in her seat and drew her eyebrows together. "Maybe just half a cup, Mother? Please? We were up quite early . . . and I feel a headache coming on. Must have been all the honking."

Miss Irene sighed but removed her hand. "I suppose one cup won't kill us. Besides, the tea water was a little hot last time," she said, frowning at the waitress. "Decaf for me, please."

Miss Irene, drinking decaf? She had a mug at home proclaiming "Death Before Decaf."

Beatrice cradled her coffee cup with both hands and held it under her nose. She closed her eyes, breathed in the heady aroma, and sighed contentedly. "I've missed your coffee, Mother. I don't know how you do it, but you've always made the best coffee."

"It's the percolator . . . ." A grin started to creep across Miss Irene's face, but she shook it away and replaced it with a frown.

"The percolator," I repeated, nodding. "What was that you told me? '*Big things perk up when the going gets hot*'?" She had once said this while winking at Big George, emphasizing the double entendre and causing J.J. to blush.

"Too much . . . . caffeine is bad for the heart," Miss Irene mumbled, pushing her cup away. She flipped the lid up on the tea pot and peered inside. "Too much hot water, too much excitement, too much . . . perking." The lid fell back with a clang. "Ridiculous. Dangerous. Irresponsible."

Beatrice sipped her coffee and grimaced. "Yes, but there's nothing in the world like a good cup of coffee."

"And this is nothing like a good cup of coffee," Vanessa said, shaking her head.

Steve shrugged. "I've had worse."

"Liar."

Steve spit a mouthful of coffee back into his cup. "You're right. This stuff is pretty vile." The two of them started giggling. Beatrice joined in.

"Back when I was in high school, we called this The Bad Way Diner," Beatrice said.

"We did too!" Vanessa replied.

Beatrice sighed. "We stopped here for breakfast after prom."

"We did too! And we bought beer at the gas station next door *before* prom."

"We did too!" Beatrice looked at her mother. "Er, um, I mean, I heard that some *other* kids did that." Miss Irene rolled her eyes.

Maybe "Bumble Bea" had inherited a little of Miss Irene's spunk after all, I thought. Maybe Beatrice wasn't the problem.

"I'm so glad you asked us to join you at your table," Beatrice said to Vanessa. "Wasn't that nice of them, mother?"

"Yes, dear. So nice." Miss Irene stared daggers at Steve. "Least they could do after riding my bumper the last ten miles."

So, she had been aware of the problems her driving caused, or at least one of them. But why had she gone from driving like she was qualifying for the Indy 500, to driving like she was 500?

"What are you up to, Miss Irene?" I leaned toward her and whispered. She had heard me whispering much quieter from much further away plenty of times when I didn't want her to hear me. Now she ignored me, a placid smile fixed beneath her vacant stare. She appeared to be every one of her 90-years-old, and then some.

"Will that be all?" The waitress asked, pulling out her order pad hopefully. As a former waitress myself, I knew free refills weren't great for tips.

"Ice cream! I'd like a hot fudge sundae, please," I blurted. Ice cream was Miss Irene's Achilles heel. If the real Miss Irene was still in there, she would never be able to resist ice cream.

"But it's not even noon yet! We'll spoil our lunch," she said.

Beatrice's face fell. "But Mother. Breakfast was . . . a little thin. And so long ago."

I decided it was time to fight dirty. "Don't forget the whipped cream."

"And you know how prompt they are at the home," Beatrice said. "If we're late – and at the rate we're going we *will* be late – Father will have already eaten."

Miss Irene bit her lip. I could sense her indecision.

"Lots. Of. Whipped. Cream." I spoke slowly, emphasizing each tempting word. Desperate times called for desperate measures.

"A scoop of frozen yogurt. Vanilla. Plain. In a bowl. Two spoons," Miss Irene finally ordered.

"Chocolate sauce on the side, please?" Beatrice asked.

The waitress nodded sympathetically. "I'll see what I can do." Then she winked at Beatrice.

"I'll have a hot fudge sundae too, please, real ice cream, whipped cream, cherry, the works," Vanessa said.

"Same here, but hold the nuts," Steve added.

"That figures." Vanessa elbowed him.

"I'm sorry, we're out of cherries," the waitress said.

"Story of your life." Steve elbowed Vanessa in return.

While we waited for our ice cream, I made up a story about needing to go to River City for a party I was planning.

"But my car is acting up," I said. "I'm not sure I should drive it that far."

"Why don't you ride with us?" Beatrice asked. "Maybe you

could drive Mom's car."

"What's wrong with . . . ." Steve started to ask me. I kicked him and he winced. "Really?" He winced again and looked toward Vanessa. "Both of you?"

"Ixnay on the questions-ay," Vanessa whispered-ish.

"Okay, first, that's not how Pig Latin works. Second, you seriously need to learn how to whisper. And third, why don't we drive your car back to Mayberry, Julie?"

The waitress returned with our ice cream before Vanessa and I could kick Steve again.

"Musta' been a mix up in the kitchen. They made up an extra sundae. Hate to let it go to waste," she said, sliding it toward Bea. She stood with her hand on her hip again and frowned at Miss Irene. "Life's short, honey, too short to waste it on boring desserts."

Miss Irene pushed her frozen yogurt around in her bowl. I noticed her looking at the pile of whipped cream on my sundae and smacking her lips. I made the most of the situation, moaning and licking my spoon.

The sugary treats lifted our spirits and loosened our tongues. We swapped mostly true stories about prom nights at The BadWay Diner, which led Beatrice to ask the probably inevitable question:

"Steve and Vanessa, you make such a cute couple. However did you meet?"

I nearly choked on a mouthful of ice cream. Steve began patting my back, not helping the situation at all, while Vanessa explained.

"Steve is, um, married to my eh-hmbm . . ." she mumbled through a mouthful of ice cream.

"I'm sorry, I didn't quite catch that last bit," Beatrice said.

"Ex-husband. Steve is married to Vanessa's ex-husband," Miss Irene said. A smile spread across her face as she watched her daughter squirm. I noticed a dollop of whipped cream at the edge of that smile, and a large chunk missing from my sundae.

Chapter 11

I knew that Miss Irene frequently visited her ex-husband Frank at the assisted living home in River City, but I had never met him. Frank's health problems slowed him down physically, but not mentally, she said. His legs were never quite the same after his mistress – Big George's wife – had accidentally hit him with a truck, putting Frank in the hospital and signaling the end of both marriages.

The lobby of Whispering River Retirement Community reminded me of the lobby of an up-scale hotel more than that of a nursing home. An attractive woman with strawberry-blond hair styled in a choppy pixie cut sat behind the semi-circular reception desk. There was a subtle "WRRC" crest on the breast pocket of her fitted jacket, and her name tag identified her as "Rita, Daytime Concierge."

"Welcome to Whispering River. Please sign our guest regis . . . . Oh! Miss Irene! I didn't recognize you!" Rita paused, and I watched her take in Miss Irene's transformation. "Mr. Truman is expecting you."

Rita looked through an arched doorway to the left of the lobby, then leaned over the desk and spoke in a quieter voice, sharing the latest gossip. "Mrs. Three stopped by early Saturday morning – unannounced – and Mrs. Four hadn't gone home Friday night! They nearly had to call security!"

Beatrice blushed. Miss Irene snorted.

"As I recall, that's how Mrs. Four *became* Mrs. Four," Miss Irene said. "Any idea where Romeo is now?"

"He's in the Great Room, auditioning applicants for Mrs. Five." Rita grinned at Miss Irene.

Beatrice sighed. "Mrs. Six. Or Six-point-five. I don't think jumpsuit Elvis was a legal officiant in Iowa. 'What happens in Vegas.' Pfft."

Rita's face went pale. "I guarantee, we supervise bus trips to the casino much closer now. *Much* closer. Things got a little crazy after he hit the big jackpot on the Wheel O' Slots machine."

"Don't you worry, dear," Miss Irene said. "Frank has always been lucky when it comes to sluts. And slots." This was the most Miss Irene-like behavior Miss Irene had shown all day. I started to think she might be getting back to normal. At least, I hoped she was.

The Great Room featured a mix of plush chairs and love seats arranged in cozy conversational groupings. A massive fireplace occupied the far corner, and along the back wall French doors led onto a patio. Frank was sitting in his wheelchair talking to two gray-haired women who were hanging on his every word.

Frank was still a good-looking man. His full head of white hair and his navy V-neck sweater, worn over a checkered shirt, emphasized his lake blue eyes. He smiled when he saw us, revealing a row of perfectly straight white teeth, which I suspected were false.

"Bonnie Bea!" he called, as Beatrice rushed into his open arms to hug him. "And . . . Irene?" he said, hesitantly. "You're looking . . . lovely. As always." He sounded like the change in Miss Irene's appearance baffled him, too.

"You must be Julie. Irene's told me so much about you." He

kissed my hand instead of shaking it. I would usually have found this creepy, but when Frank did it, it seemed gallant.

Frank's two admirers reluctantly surrendered their sofa to Miss Irene and Beatrice. I sat catty-corner to them in a barrel-back chair.

"Forgive me for asking, Irene, my dear, but there's something . . . different about you. A new hairstyle, perhaps?" Frank gave me a sideways glance and raised an eyebrow questioningly. I shrugged.

"I thought it might be time for a change," Miss Irene said sharply. I noticed she avoided making eye contact with him.

"Ahh, yes. Change." He nodded slowly as he continued to examine her. "Change can be a good thing. Although not when done to please someone else, I've heard. And how is George doing?"

"He's fine."

"Frightening business, his little trip to the hospital." Frank prompted. Miss Irene inhaled sharply and pulled at the cuff of her cardigan. "But if I know George, he isn't letting it slow him down."

"He was back at the shop this morning," I said.

Miss Irene looked up at me, her eyes open wide in alarm. "Oh, dear. I hope J.J. isn't letting him overdo it."

"I'm sure he'll be fine dear. J.J. loves him almost as much as you do." Frank's gaze never wavered from her face. "George is a lucky man. He has a family who loves him, and work he loves to do. Those are the things that keep a body young. We see it all the time here – new residents join us, thinking of nothing but leisure. They lose their drive, their zest. Then poof!" Frank sighed and sank into his chair. "Such a waste."

"Daddy's the unofficial activity director here at Whispering River," Beatrice said proudly.

"It's not much different than sales, when you get right down to it. I'm trying to get folks to invest in their future. Although not in so many words. Turns out I have a gift for reading people." Frank looked at Miss Irene and frowned, then turned his attention to me.

"Take you for example, Julie." He took my hands in his, then stared into my eyes. He tilted his head to the left and then the right. "Hmm, hmm. Yes. Indeed. I think you'd be interested in our musical programs. You're in luck! Dale Thomas will be playing for us this afternoon." Frank smiled, then turned my hands over and studied my palms. "Ahh. Of course, you need to feel needed. You could help organize our mixers, perhaps chaperone our day trips and bus rides. And a fitness buff, I see. Perhaps you could volunteer for our bicycle taxi program, help our residents get a little fresh air. It's not quite the same as riding The Scout, of course, but . . . ."

"You old shyster!" Miss Irene interrupted. "I told you all about Joe, Julie's job, and The Scout!"

"Ahh. There's my girl! You never were one for subterfuge." Frank grinned and sat back in his seat again. He seemed as pleased as I was to see the spunky side of Miss Irene. "Indeed, my dear, you are correct. I simply draw from all the resources available to me."

Frank had arranged for a private lunch on the patio and secured "the finest table in the house" for the musical performance. If I hadn't felt like the other women were constantly sizing me up as competition for Frank's affection, it would have been fun. After post-concert coffee and dessert –

with Dale himself – we made our way back to the lobby and said our goodbyes.

"The next time I see you will be at the wedding," Frank said. Miss Irene didn't reply. "I don't suppose you'd consider letting me give the bride away, would you? Although, if I was smart, I would never have let you go the first time." Miss Irene rolled her eyes – another spark, I thought. "Ah well, with age comes wisdom."

"Sometimes," Miss Irene whispered.

"I look forward to celebrating a lifetime of love, the love of a lifetime . . . a love that gives you life. Hmmm. I might have to use that for my toast. Try to act surprised when I say it, won't you, dear?"

Beatrice hugged her father once more, then she and Miss Irene walked to the door. Frank gently put his hand on my arm, holding me back until they were outside.

"Keep on eye on her, Julie. She's . . . well, you know. Once Irene sets her mind to something, she can be . . . determined. Keep an eye on her."

When we got back to Pleasant Glen, my Mini Cooper was in the driveway, but the garage stall where The Scout was usually parked was still empty. A light was on in Miss Irene's kitchen and I could see Big George sitting at the table. Miss Irene's newly acquired little old lady shuffle was forgotten as she rushed to the house.

"Good evening, ladies! I trust all went well in River City? Quite a coincidence, you all meeting up at the diner, hmmm?" Big George crossed his arms and frowned at me. "Vanessa told me all about it." I had no doubt that Vanessa had melted like an ice pop in hell under George's interrogation. I was going to owe her big for this one. In the meantime, though, I was feeling the heat myself. I decided the best defense was a good offense and tried to switch the subject.

"So, how'd it go with The Scout today?" I asked.

Big George shook his head. "She's being contrary. There are no obvious leaks, plugs, shorts or loose wires. 'Course I only had time for a superficial examination. After you left, J.J. put me in charge of customer relations while he hid out in the shop. He said I was the one who caused this mess, so I could deal with it." I thought Big George looked amused.

"What was J.J. thinking?" Miss Irene slammed her hand down on the table. "What were *you* thinking, George? You should have stayed home today. The doctor told you to take it easy." Miss Irene spun in her chair to vent her fury at me. "What were *you* thinking, Julie? Bothering George like that? The Scout is getting to be more trouble than she's worth. Some days I just think . . . maybe you kids were right, Bea. Maybe it's time to sell her. She's an old relic. Too old to be out on the streets."

Beatrice looked at Big George and I watched the color drain from her cheeks. "But . . . no! Mom, that's not . . . I mean, she's . . . you're . . . ."

"Pah! Just a silly, old, hunk of metal. Don't know why I've held on to it for this long. Maybe they'll take it up at that museum." Miss Irene stormed from the kitchen, the swinging door flapping behind her. We all watched in silence.

"George, that's not . . . she can't . . . ." Beatrice's voice was barely more than a whisper, her eyes filled with tears and her lip trembled.

"I know, Bumble Bea. I know." George reached out and took Bea's hand in his, but his eyes never left the door.

Chapter 12

In the middle of all that excitement, I missed a phone call from Joe. This was nothing new, unfortunately. Between constantly changing schedules, background noise, and poor connections, we relied on text and voicemail when Joe was on the road. He was a great message leaver, working in snippets of songs that fit the situation perfectly. That night it was Billy Joel's "Sometimes a Fantasy." I was starting to think that was our theme song. There was good news, though. Joe's schedule had changed – yet again – and the meeting was moved – yet again – giving him a 24-hour layover in Iowa the next day.

His plane was originally scheduled to arrive at 11 a.m., so – of course – take off was delayed. I took advantage of the extra hour to check in at Pleasant Glen Cycles and Motors before leaving for the airport. Miss Irene had reluctantly agreed to let Big George go in to work, as long as he stayed out front greeting customers. So – of course – I found him in the shop, sleeves rolled up, grease up to his elbows, performing open heart surgery on The Scout.

"I still haven't been able to pinpoint the problem, Julie," Big George said, shaking his head. "I've decided to give her the full works – I'm draining her fluids, cleaning the carbs, changing the plugs and filters, checking the seals and bearings." He grinned and gently patted her leather saddle, which was protected by a clean, red, cotton shop cloth. "Spending some quality time with her. It's a regular spa day. Got the idea from you girls. Miss

Irene is looking forward to her 'Posh and Polish' day before the wedding. It'll be good for her." A worried look replaced his grin. He patted The Scout's saddle more slowly. "Least I hope so." So did I.

Joe's rescheduled flight arrived right on rescheduled time. I watched as he made his way unnoticed through the terminal. At one point, a woman wearing an Average Joe's concert t-shirt bumped into him. "Ope! Sorry," she said, not giving him a second glance.

"How do you do that?" I asked him after a very welcoming "welcome home" kiss.

"Well, I can't explain it, but I'd be happy to demonstrate again."

"Not that," I said – after another kiss, of course. "I mean, how do you walk through a crowd totally unnoticed?"

"It's my superpower. And this hardly counts as a crowd." He flashed me that megawatt, rock-star grin, and caught "Ope, sorry" lady in the flashover. Her suitcase took another trip around the baggage carousel as she stared at Joe, trying to decide if she recognized him. I watched as she scanned him top to bottom, taking in the Hawkeye baseball cap pulled low on his forehead, his gray t-shirt proudly proclaiming "Iowa," and the faded jeans that fit just right. Then she glanced around at the other men standing there – most of whom were dressed just like him – shook her head and meandered toward the exit. She looked back over her shoulder twice but didn't stop.

"Close call there, Clark Kent," I said to Joe.

"What can I say? You're my kryptonite, Lois." We made it to the car without further incident. As we pulled out of the parking lot, Joe reached over and gently traced my jaw with his finger. I nearly rear-ended a tractor. Talk about your kryptonite.

"I have one request," he said, grinning suggestively.

"Holing up in a hotel room instead of driving all the way to Pleasant Glen?"

"Good idea, but unfortunately no. Let's take the old county road down to River City. After all that L.A. traffic, I've had enough concrete. I need to see some open fields."

"Joe, darling, this is Iowa. The *interstate* is surrounded by fields. *Everything* is surrounded by fields."

"I know. I'm just ready to slow down."

The further we got from the highway – the longer we were surrounded by fields – the more relaxed Joe became. He held my hand, sank back into his seat and looked out the window, commenting on the progress of the harvest, the geese on the Iowa River, and the urban sprawl.

Rubbie's Cycles on the edge of River City grabbed his attention. The massive warehouse of a building was covered in glittering stainless-steel letters advertising motorcycles, ATVs, and personal watercraft. "That's a bit different than J.J.'s shop," he said, chuckling.

"You have no idea." Joe raised one eyebrow, encouraging me to explain. "I stopped in there soon after I got my motorcycle license. I love The Scout, but I just wanted to see what else was available."

"You should have been able to find something there."

"They have a little bit of everything – shirts, jackets, boots, glassware, key chains, accessories. They even have a bar that serves craft beer, artisan whiskey and imported cigars. If you look really hard, you might find a few motorcycles tucked in around the edges."

"Hmm, not quite J.J.'s marketing plan. Did you find anything?"

"When I finally got a salesman's attention and convinced him I wasn't shopping for my boyfriend, he tried to sell me an underpowered scooter with a metallic purple paint job."

"And you let him live?" Joe laughed.

"Well, I'd just had the car detailed, and I didn't know where I'd stash the body. And it was a *sparkly* purple. Came with a pink helmet."

"Does J.J. know about this?"

"No, and he doesn't need to know, either. It made me realize how spoiled I am. J.J. may be annoying sometimes, but at least he treats me like I have a brain." All this talk about secrets and J.J. reminded me of the Vincent.

"So, have you ever thought about getting a motorcycle?" I asked, trying to sound casual.

Joe turned to look at the fields again, but continued to rub his thumb across the back of my hand. "No, not really," he said, shaking his head slowly. "You know what I *have* been thinking about?" He leaned over and whispered in my ear. "I mean, besides you and tonight." When he kissed my neck, I almost ran us off the road.

"A hamburger and fries from The Cap," he said. He kissed me again. "And a milkshake."

I got the distinct impression he was trying to distract me. But damn, he did a good job of it.

Chapter 13

Old Capitol Burgers is as well-known for the wait to get a table there as it is for its burgers and shakes. Joe and I got to The Cap at 1:30, just in time to stand in line with all the other people who thought they would miss the lunch crowd. After fifteen minutes of waiting, we had moved from standing just outside the doorway, to standing just inside the doorway. There were still three groups of diners ahead of us. Outside, the smell of hamburgers on the grill had teased us. Inside, a parade of frosty, stainless steel blender cups and the hiss and pop of french fries in the deep fryer tempted us. We distracted ourselves from the agonizing wait by studying the list of homemade pies – served *à la mode* or *mixed into a milkshake*! There was no way I was leaving before I had a rhubarb pie shake.

"I don't suppose you could turn off your rock star cloak of invisibility long enough to get us bumped to the front of the line, could you?" I asked Joe. I leaned in close to him so we could talk to each other without being overheard. And because I liked to lean in close to him.

"That wouldn't be fair, now would it? Besides, I don't think it works that way. There's a chance I'm not as well-known as you think I am. It's not like I'm Dan Gable."

At the mention of the former Iowa wrestling coach's name, the people on either side of us craned their necks to scan the crowd. They whispered to the people next to them, and soon everyone in line was checking not just to see which table might be leaving soon, but also whether Gable was actually there.

"See what you started?" Joe whispered to me. "Your confidence in me does wonders for my ego. Everybody should have someone who makes them feel like they are the center of the universe."

"You underestimate yourself. Millions of concert goers can't be wrong."

"That's not the same thing. I mean, it's nice, and I wouldn't have a job if people didn't buy tickets. But when the stage lights go out, or when I'm walking through the airport, or standing in line for a table . . . ." Joe shrugged. "You're the one that makes me feel important, Julie. You're the only one I need to hear shouting my name. Especially when the lights go out and we're . . . ." Joe's lips brushed my ear sending goosebumps down my spine. Joe's kisses were almost enough to make me forget about rhubarb pie shakes. Before I could change my mind about the wait, a woman's voice cut through the chatter and the clatter of silverware on heavy china.

"Joe? Joe Davenport? Get over here, little lamb!"

"Looks like you got your wish," Joe grinned. The other people waiting in line grumbled at our sudden good fortune, even as they tried to figure out where they'd heard that name before. We weaved our way through the narrow dining area to the back of the room, where a high-backed booth provided a semi-private nook.

"The lost has been found! Mary's little lamb has returned!" The woman wrapped Joe in a hug, then stepped back and shook her head. Long streamers of silver curls cascaded over her shoulders. "Just look at you! You can pluck the boy off the farm, but he ain't never gonna change, no sir!"

Joe kissed her cheek. "Mary, Mary, Quite Contrary," he said, affectionately.

"Aw, no one's called me that in years!" Mary laughed, setting her entire body in motion.

"Not to her face, anyways." Mary's lunch companion unfolded himself from the cramped booth to shake Joe's hand. "Good to see you man."

Joe put his arm around me. "Tom, Mary, this is Julie. Julie, this is Tom and Mary Shepherd."

Tom was tall and thin, making Mary look short and plump by comparison. His pale skin contrasted starkly against his black jeans, shirt and porkpie hat. Mary was a riot of color – her skin glowed red-brown like burnished copper and her flowing, jewel-toned kaftan brushed the top of gorgeous, iridescent cowboy boots.

"Julie! It's so nice to meet you dear!" Mary took both my hands in hers and gave them a gentle squeeze. She gazed at me until I ducked my head and blushed.

"Don't scare the girl, Mare," Tom drawled. "Nice to meet you, Julie." He bowed and tipped his hat.

"Sit down, sit down! This gives me a reason to order a slice of pie!" Mary shooed us into the booth and waved a waitress over.

"Mary and Tom gave me my first big break when they let me sit in with Mary and the Blues Shepherds out at the state fair," Joe said.

"Oh sure, blame it all on us," Tom grinned.

"Hush now," Mary swatted Tom's arm. "Joe was just a baby, Julie. Skinny little white boy, fresh off the farm!"

"I was seventeen, showing 4-H cattle at the fair. At night, I'd slip out of the Youth Inn and prowl around, taking in all the bands. Nobody thought twice about one more guy in jeans and a t-shirt hanging around with the stage crews."

"Ballsy, too," Tom said. "One minute he was running cables, the next he was sitting at the piano."

"I recognized a couple of the Shepherds gettin' drunk at the Stockman's Inn," Joe shrugged. "I figured at the very least they'd miss sound check."

"This lamb was sitting there all sweet and innocent when Rollie and Mike stumbled to the stage. Mike put one foot on those steps and boom! Down he went. Passed out, cold," Mary shook her head, causing the waves to tumble. "Joe says 'I could sit in, if you'd like,' then he gives me that grin of his. I figured if nothin' else, he'd be good eye candy for the ladies. 'Course I didn't know then how young he was."

"Like fun you didn't, woman! Always did go for younger men." Tom winked at me.

"Fifteen years doesn't seem like much now . . . ."

"I'd be more worried if Julie here wasn't so pretty."

"Oh no you don't. I just got her back. I'm not about to let her go again," Joe said, putting his arm around my shoulders. Mary glanced at Tom, then continued her story.

"Anyway, that grin just sealed the deal. I decided to take a chance on him. The Shepherds all agreed."

"Not *all* of them," Joe said.

"Well, no, Rollie was a bit put out," Mary admitted.

"Then you launched into 'Mary Had A Little Lamb' like Buddy Guy himself traded his guitar for a piano," Tom said. "I thought Rollie'd stroke out – that had always been his signature song. Pissed him off to no end when Stevie Ray Vaughan started playin' it."

"You two boys always was at loggerheads," Mary said. "Rollie needed someone to keep him on his toes."

Joe frowned. "Cocky bastard."

"Aw, Joe. He had the talent. He just never knew how to channel his energy. I don't suppose you've . . . ." Mary let the question hang.

"No. Not for years now. Not since . . . ." Joe sighed and pushed his plate away.

"Well, Rollie always did what he thought was best for Rollie. He'll turn up."

"A bad penny always does," Tom muttered.

"Speaking of turning up, what brings you back to this side of the state, Joe? We began to think you were avoiding us!"

"Yeah, well, for a while there, Eastern Iowa kinda lost its appeal for me." Joe grinned at me. "But the more I'm here, the more I like it. I'm just back for the day. A little business, a little pleasure."

"You're in luck! The band's gettin' together at our house tonight."

"Now, Tom. Joe might have better things . . . ."

"What could be better than . . . ."

"Joe *and Julie* might have better things to do . . . ." Mary clarified.

"I appreciate the offer, but Julie and I do have plans. Maybe next time . . . ."

I saw how Joe's eyes lit up when Tom mentioned the get together. It was obvious that he wanted to go. Besides, listening to them reminisce reminded me of how much I still had to learn about Joe's history.

"Your flight doesn't leave until 10 tomorrow, right honey? And you'll be back Thursday night?"

"Well, that's the plan, but . . . ."

"I think I can share you for a few hours. Besides, Bob's always talking about when Mary and The Blues Shepherds used to play at The Bar, but I've never heard you." I had avoided The Bar after Joe left all those years ago and missed out on a lot of extraordinary music.

"You know that old scalawag? We haven't played The Bar in a dog's age. Oh, the stories I could tell!" Mary said.

"I guess it's all set then!" Joe's broad smile assured me I had made the right decision. He leaned over to kiss my cheek. "Thank you, honey. You are the center of my universe."

Truth is, I love watching Joe play the piano almost as much as I love spending time alone with him. There is something about the way he becomes one with the music that I find magical. And incredibly sexy. It isn't just the smile on his face, or the way he bites his lip when he concentrates, or even the way he closes his eyes and throws his head back when he sings. I can feel the joy radiating off him, warm and electric.

That night at Tom and Mary's was no exception. Joe looked like he was having a great time playing and swapping stories. I had a great time, laughing at the stories, listening to the music, and watching Joe enjoy himself. But I felt like an outsider. I could listen, I could laugh, but I had nothing to contribute. So, when Mary started gathering up dishes, I jumped at the chance to help.

"A good hostess would say no. But I'm a *smart* hostess," Mary said. Even her laugh was musical – warm and slightly breathy like the sound of the Hammond B3 organ in her living room that Joe was playing. "I haven't seen Joe this happy since he met a certain waitress, way back when." I felt myself starting to blush. "I don't know what happened and I don't *want* to know. I'm just glad to see my little lamb happy again. You are a special woman, Julie. Joe loves you very much."

"I love him, too, Mary. I always have." I wiped absentmindedly at a plate.

"But?" Mary must have sensed something in my silence.

"But . . . coordinating our two lives is a little harder than I expected it would be."

"What do you mean, baby?"

"His music, I mean, his career as a musician. There's just so much I don't understand. I don't know how I fit in. It's like he has this whole other life without me."

"What did Joe say when you told him how you felt?"

"That's part of the problem." I shrugged. "Joe's been traveling so much that when we are in the same place at the same time, we . . . tend to get distracted."

Mary laughed again. "There's nothing wrong with a little distraction now and then! Lord knows it's saved my marriage more than once. Sometimes a good distraction says more than words ever could – *I love you, I need you, I'm sorry.*" Mary handed me another plate. "It's been a long time since Joe has had someone to share his life with. That trampy, little manager doesn't count. You're going to have to help him, honey. If there's somethin' bothering you, speak up. He'll come around. Meanwhile, enjoy the distractions and just keep on doin' what you're doin'."

"All I'm doin' is sitting around listening."

"Oh honey, that's all he needs. You've seen him on stage. You've seen the look on his face when he connects with the audience. That's nothing compared to the look he gets when you're there. We've played with Joe plenty of times, but tonight? Mmmm-hmmm. Tonight, he was *on*. And we was just messing around.

"He loves you Julie. I can see it on his face, and I can hear it in his music. He loves you just the way you are. Huh. Maybe he should write a song about that. Maybe someone already did! That boy loves you for *who* you are, not *what* you are or what you can do for him."

"Thank you, Mary."

"Don't thank me! You'll make me feel guilty for leaving you here to wash dishes while I go out there and check on the boys." Mary dried her hands thoughtfully "Just between you and me, honey, I love my Tom, but sometimes we need a little more separation between our married life and our business life. You two will figure it out. Talk to him, Julie. Joe's a good man."

Mary was right. Stewing about things wouldn't solve the problem. As soon as we got back to my apartment, Joe and I needed to talk. *Without* getting distracted.

I was rinsing the last of the suds out of the sink when I heard the door open again. I felt goosebumps on the back of my neck and knew without turning around that it was Joe, not Mary, who walked up behind me. My suspicion was confirmed when he wrapped his arms around my waist and kissed that spot just below my ear. I remembered what Mary said about a little distraction never hurting anyone.

The band was playing a funky, blues groove in the other room. Joe moved his hands to my hips, and we started to sway. The tempo was slow and seductive. Tom was singing in a gravel-rough voice.

"I don't think I know this song. But I like it," I said.

"Buddy Guy. 'What Kind of Woman Is This'." Joe kissed my ear. "Maybe it's time for us to go," he whispered.

"Maybe," I said, leaning back against him. There was nothing wrong with a little distraction, but I didn't want Joe to think I could be distracted that easily.

"Maybe?" Joe's breath was warm against my neck. "Maybe I should try harder." He trailed kisses down my neck to my shoulder. Who was I kidding? Of course I could be distracted that easily!

"Maybe we *should* go," I mumbled, turning to wrap my arms around his neck. Seriously? Who could blame me for being distracted? Those eyes! Those lips! Those hands! Those hips!

"Maybe," he chuckled. Instead of leaving, Joe eased me back to that sexy sway.

On any given day Joe can melt my panties with just a look. Now, hypnotized by the slow and steady tempo of the music, the sensual *boom . . . snick* of the drums, the keening guitar, I was ready to spontaneously combust. As we swayed and kissed, my heartbeat pounded in my ears, blocking out the music, blocking out the clapping . . . .

Blocking out the clapping?

Joe and I froze. Caught up in our . . . distraction, we hadn't noticed the music end. We hadn't noticed the kitchen door swing open. We hadn't noticed we had an audience standing in the doorway until the slow clapping began.

Joe rested his forehead against mine. "Tom?" he whispered.

I peeked over Joe's shoulder. "And Mary," I whispered in reply.

"That, ladies and gentlemen, is how baby grands are made," Tom said.

"Lord love a duck! Leave those kids alone, Tom."

"Why don't you kiss me like that anymore?"

"Why don't you help me with the dishes anymore? What is wrong with you? These two are in love."

"Um, we should probably be, um . . . ." I mumbled, looking at them over Joe's shoulder.

"Blah, blah, blah. It was a lovely evening, but you need to get going. I understand. If someone would kiss me like that, I'd get going too," Tom said, winking at Mary.

"Look what you two started!" Mary pushed Tom back into the living room. "You have definitely got to come 'round here more often. Mmm, hmm." She followed Tom, singing "The House Is A Rockin'."

Joe and I let ourselves out the backdoor. I doubt that even Miss Irene could have kept up with me as I raced to Pleasant Glen. Once we made it to my apartment, we picked up where we left off, and I let Joe distract me all night long.

Chapter 14

After a night filled with plenty of distractions and very little discussion, I reluctantly drove Joe back to the airport. This time, unfortunately, his flight left right on time.

As soon as I got back to Pleasant Glen, I stopped in to check on Big George and The Scout. I entered the shop through an open garage door, ignoring the "Employees Only" sign. The crew was at lunch, leaving Big George alone with The Scout. Big George sat on a short, wheeled stool, one hand rubbing the top of her gas tank absentmindedly while he examined her engine. The overhead shop lights cast bruise-like shadows on The Scout, and Big George looked worried. His lips were moving, but I couldn't tell if he was muttering to himself or whispering to The Scout.

"Obstinate, headstrong woman," he said, abruptly pushing his stool back.

"I don't understand it, Julie-dear. I've gone over her from stem to stern and I can't find anything wrong. I've drained, cleaned and replaced everything that can be drained, cleaned or replaced, but something's still off." His shoulders slumped. "It seems neither of my girls will talk to me."

"So, Miss Irene is still . . . not feeling herself?"

"The source of her ailment, like the source of The Scout's, continues to elude me. That woman has never had a headache in her life, much less . . . ."

"She'll come around. They both will," I said, although I was starting to worry, too. As far as I knew, Big George had tried everything short of a séance to get The Scout running again. If I thought a séance would do the trick, I'd bring the candles and chicken feet.

A delivery boy from PeeGee's bakery came in from the office area carrying a bag. I figured things must be pretty bad if J.J. was resorting to delivery instead of picking up lunch himself. Then I recognized the scowl beneath the low-pulled baseball cap and sunglasses. It took J.J. a little longer to recognize me.

"Hey! Employees only . . . . Oh. It's just you, Julie," he said, taking off the sunglasses. "I ran into Muffy earlier this morning. She thinks she – and I quote – 'needs her headlights adjusted,' so I told her to stop by this afternoon. I thought you were . . . ." I knew I looked a little tired after last night, but being mistaken for Muffy? That hurt. "Anyway, would you keep an eye out for her, Dad? Seems like that service call is right up your alley."

I expected Big George to reprimand J.J. for what I thought was a rude comment. When he said nothing, I leapt to defend his honor, as well as Muffy's. "Hey! She might have a serious . . . ."

"Oh, please! You wouldn't believe the number of headlights and wax jobs I've been asked to look at lately. And if one more person offers to check my dipstick, so help me . . . ." He thrust the bag at his dad. "By the way, Miss Irene got to Velma. Salads with low-fat dressing for both of us."

J.J. stomped back to the door leading to the offices but seemed to lose steam along the way. He paused, hand on the door knob. "Rumor has it Muffy's husband has moved out," he said without turning around. "Check the wiring to her headlights, then check her alternator." He let the door slam shut behind him.

"I take it the whole Studly McStudlyson thing is wearing on

him?" I asked.

"It's slowing down, I think," Big George said. He examined his lunch bag. "No phone numbers today. Apparently, there's a fine line between playing hard to get, and playing impossible to get."

"So, I shouldn't tease him about it?"

"Of course you should. But not today. Give him some time, my dear. He's taking this pretty seriously. More seriously than Miss Irene and I ever did. Tales of our . . . exploits may have been exaggerated. You know how Pleasant Glen loves a good rumor."

Big George rolled his chair over to the work counter and cleared off a space for his lunch. He spoke slowly, choosing his words carefully. "Making love to someone involves more than just intercourse. I hope J.J. can find that – again. He needs someone to look after him. We all do. Even if it isn't always what we want." He took a styrofoam box out of the bag and opened it. "Salad, with grilled chicken and low-fat dressing." He sighed.

"Do you want me to try to sneak a burger for you?"

"We tried that yesterday. Your name is probably on the 'do not feed' list, as well, my dear. Irene's intentions are good. I guess." Big George glanced at the door to the office area again. "Could you talk to J.J. for me? I may not have handled this in the best way for him."

The door to J.J.'s office was closed and the window blinds were down. I knocked, but he didn't respond. This whole pouting/recluse thing had gone on long enough, as far as I was concerned. And I was still angry about being mistaken for Muffy. Big George wanted me to talk some sense into him? I'd be happy to.

As I opened the door to J.J.'s office I had an uncomfortable flashback to the night I had opened my bedroom door to find

Gary – very much my husband at that moment – in bed with Vanessa – very much *not* my best friend at that moment. The scene in J.J.'s office shocked me almost as badly. I quickly shut the door behind me.

"What the heck do you think you're doing?" I hissed.

"Julie! I can explain. This isn't what it looks like." He looked down at the enormous hamburger in his hands. "Of course it is! I'm having lunch, for goodness' sake." He paused before taking another bite. "Big George isn't with you, is he?"

"No. He's out in the shop eating his salad. I thought you said you both had salads!"

"Lettuce, pickle, onion and tomato." J.J. talked as he chewed. "Salad-ish."

"I thought you said, and I quote, 'Miss Irene got to Velma'."

"She did. Lucky for me Tiffany was working the counter."

"But Miss Irene is worried about your health."

"Miss Irene is worried about *Big George's* health. *I'm* just fine."

"You won't be when Big George finds out!"

"I'll share my fries." J.J. turned the to-go box towards me in an unspoken bribe. Velma cuts the potatoes for her french fries by hand each morning and fries them up in a secret blend of oils that probably contains enough trans and saturated fats to give you a heart attack just by thinking of them. They are, without a doubt, the most delicious french fries available in Pleasant Glen. I would wager that many a person's silence had been bought with Velma's fries throughout the years.

"Deal," I said, reaching for the box. "But I feel dirty."

"Me too. I feel so guilty I almost can't enjoy this burger." He stuffed a wad of fries in his mouth and closed his eyes while he chewed. "But these fries are worth it."

J.J. rearranged the tomato and pickle on his burger. "I understand how Miss Irene feels. I never thought about Big George's mortality before. But since the hospital? That's all I can think about. He's ninety years old, Julie. Ninety! I used to think age was just a number. But now?"

"What is it you teach the newbies in Miss Irene's Finishing School? Does 'never judge someone's abilities by their appearances' sound familiar?" For many years, PGC&M had hired high schoolers for summer work, paying them for what was essentially community service. The youngsters learned good manners in addition to work skills.

J.J. shook his head. "That's appearance, not age. Big George doesn't look a day over eighty and acts even younger. But he's ninety, Julie. *Nine-Dee*. Heck, he's almost *nine-dee-one*." J.J. tossed the rest of his burger back into the box and closed it. "Anyway, it's not his appearance, or his age. He's struggling. You saw him out there in the shop. I've never seen him have this much trouble with *any* bike, much less The Scout."

J.J. pushed the box of fries toward me, but I had lost my appetite.

"Maybe it's not Big George that's the problem," I mumbled.

"I hope not. He's still my best mechanic, Julie. How he's kept The Scout running as well as he has for as long as he has is beyond me. But look at it this way – what if it *is* The Scout and not him? What if he can't get her running again? What's that going to do to him? What's that going to do to Miss Irene? To you? You're all caught up in that crazy hoodoo – talking to The Scout like she's a real person, giving her credit for changing your life." My eyes filled with tears and I started to sniffle.

"Christ on a cracker!" J.J. rummaged around in his lunch bag and handed me a wad of napkins, keeping one for himself. "I'm just sayin', maybe you all should start preparing yourselves. Maybe it would be better for everyone if you let Miss Irene donate The Scout to the museum. The more Dad struggles to get her running, the harder it is on him.

"It might be time to admit that The Scout's best riding days may be behind her. It might be time to consider a new ride."

I nodded my head.

"I have an entire showroom of bright, shiny toys out there for you to choose from."

I opened the door and took a deep breath.

"I could even have one painted metallic purple for you." I should have known I couldn't keep that a secret. I tried to stifle a giggle, which caused me to snort, which caused me to blow a colossal snot bubble. Great. I managed to escape the ugly cry, but there's no way to pretty-up a snot bubble.

"Asshat." I whispered.

"Maybe I can special order a hot pink helmet."

"Watch it, Studly McStudlyson. I may give Muffy your private number." I stuck my tongue out at J.J. for good measure, then left his door wide open and stormed off to the showroom. I hope Big George caught him with his fries open.

I usually enjoy checking out new bikes, but I was worried about The Scout. I prowled the showroom half-heartedly, like a family member browsing in the hospital gift shop while they wait to hear how surgery went.

Pleasant Glen Cycles and Motors' inventory is small, but top quality. J.J. stocks a few new Harleys, Hondas and Yamahas – bikes that are surefire sellers, but which are available at many area retailers. The gently used bikes he carries represent the more exotic – at least in Iowa – brands. J.J. thinks of himself as a "sales facilitator," working with a network of sellers and seekers who share an appreciation for BMWs, Nortons, Triumphs, Iowa-made but relatively rare Victories, Ducatis, and, of course, truly vintage bikes.

There were plenty of, as J.J. said, "shiny toys," but nothing that compared to The Scout. My heart just wasn't in this. Maybe I'd let J.J. pick something for me. I was walking back toward his office when I noticed a motorcycle off by itself in the corner, hidden in shadow. Propped on its side stand, it leaned against the wall like a leather-clad bad boy, cool and aloof.

It was a cafe racer – J.J. had taught me a lot – with lean, minimalist bodywork. The short fairing and low handlebars reminded me of heavy-lidded, bedroom eyes. The recessed knee grips on the fuel tank looked like chiseled cheekbones. The glossy, midnight blue paint added to its swarthy good looks. The footrests were set back and the pipes were upswept, like a pair of long, lanky legs. The slim, short bench seat hugged the bike like a snug pair of chinos stretched across a high, tight . . . seat. As I stepped closer, the shadows shifted, revealing subtle gold script on the tank. *Moto Guzzi.*

A voice in my head whispered *"Ciao, bella."*
Paolo.

I gasped in recognition, transported back in time. Back to my college days – before Joe, before Gary. Vanessa and I had gone to The Club House, one of the most popular college bars in downtown River City. The upstairs was crazy-packed. All the balcony tables overlooking the crowded dance floor were taken. We merged with the flow of traffic and were swept along downstairs. Vanessa joined a queue at the bar, and I pressed on to an overlooked space tucked beneath the stairs. There, in a relatively quiet corner, I found a table.

And Paolo.

Paolo slouched casually against the back wall. He was built like a soccer player, tall and slender. Every well-defined muscle and bulge was visible beneath his tight chinos. Two extra buttons were unbuttoned, European style, on his silk-blend shirt. It would have looked cheesy on another man, but on Paolo it looked delicious, revealing his perfectly formed, tanned, hairless chest.

"*Ciao, bella,*" he said. When he smiled, his luscious lips revealed blindingly white teeth. He told me he was from Italy, studying at the university. And that may have even been true. I was so taken in by his brown-black eyes, and thick, slicked-back hair that he could have told me he was a serial killer and I wouldn't have cared. Those tight chinos and flat abs could excuse a multitude of sins. And sinning was exactly what I had on my mind.

He flirted with me for at least five minutes before Vanessa extricated herself from the scrum of State U football players who were professing their undying devotion and singing "You've Lost That Loving Feeling" to her. When she found us, the natural order of things was restored, and I was relegated to "hot girl's friend with a great personality." I spent the rest of the night talking to Paolo's frat brother, Harvey, from Council Bluffs – another "friend with great personality."

After a pitcher of boysenberry kamikazes and a couple slow dances, Vanessa gave the prearranged signal. She and I left the bar – alone – and stopped at Rocky Rococo's for a slice of pizza before making the long drive back to Pleasant Glen.

Alone.

Vanessa said she could never date a boy who was more high maintenance than she was. No matter how good he smelled. I thought I'd like to give it a try.

"*Ciao, bello,*" I whispered to the Guzzi, reaching out to touch it.

"Ohhhhh, no. No, no, no. No." J.J. took me by the elbow, turning me away from the Moto Guzzi and back toward the center of the showroom. "No." He said again. Firmly.

"But . . . ."

"No. End of discussion."

"I was just . . . ."

"Oh, I know what you were 'just.' And the answer is no. You are not riding that Guzzi. I might as well just dress you in a negligee, hand you a bottle of Jack and drop you off on Capitol Hill. The answer is no."

"Do I need to put you two in a timeout?" Big George walked into the showroom wiping his hands on a shop rag. He looked tired and distracted. I guessed things were still not going well with The Scout.

"He won't let me see Paolo. I mean, the Moto Guzzi." Even I thought that sounded whiny. I didn't care. "He thinks it's too sexy for me."

"I never said that."

"I'm sure that's not what . . . ." Big George tried to calm me.

"You can't judge a person's . . . ."

"And that's true, but . . . ." Big George interrupted.

"Not this again!" J.J. interrupted Big George's interruption.

"Stop it. Both of you." Big George said, stepping between us. "She's right, son. You shouldn't make judgments based on appearances. But you have." *Ha!* "You both have." *Huh?*

I took a deep breath and prepared to argue. J.J. looked like he wasn't ready to back down, either. Big George held up his hands to stop us.

"J.J., you are concerned about putting an attractive woman on an attractive motorcycle. But you are completely overlooking Julie's competence as a rider." J.J. hung his head.

"And Julie, what was it about this bike in particular that appealed to you?"

"Well, he – it . . . ." *Crap.*

"This isn't some brooding Italian playboy. It is a powerful machine, built for performance." I hung my head.

"You are both focusing on the appearance of this motorcycle. I'll agree. It is very stylish – some might even say sexy. But you are missing the bigger picture." Big George broke into an enormous grin. "This bike was built for fun. You both need to lighten up and enjoy life. You can't control what other people think, or how they act. The best you can do is to love them and accept them for who they are. Stop judging them for what they are, what they ride – or even how old they are.

"Now, if you'll excuse me, I have a few more things to try on The Scout. After all, if I can make you two listen to reason, getting through to The Scout and Miss Irene should be a piece of cake." Big George headed back to the shop with a confident spring in his step. He stopped and turned back to us when he reached the door.

"And by the way, son, you might want to wipe that ketchup off your chin. Tomorrow we trade lunches."

Chapter 15

Getting dumped by Paolo turned out to be the highlight of my day. Back at my apartment, I had just nuked a cardboard-flavored, low-cal meal when Helen called. She had gone to Des Moines with Gary but called Miss Irene daily to check up on Big George. After they spoke, Helen called me to check up on Miss Irene.

"She sounds so tired and . . . old," Helen said. "There's none of that trademark Irene spunk or sparkle that makes her so charismatic."

"And by 'charismatic,' I take it you mean endearing, eccentric and embarrassing?" I asked.

"Naturally."

These calls also gave Helen an excuse to tell me all about Gary's "adorable condo" in a "trendy, yet safe" neighborhood on the west side of town. When she turned on all her real estate sales charm it was almost enough to make me consider moving. Inevitably, she would sigh and fret about Gary's struggle to adapt to life on his own.

"I'm trying to help him, Julie, but you know men. Left to their own devices they revert to college dorm décor. I half expect to walk in some day and find a Farrah Fawcett poster hanging over the fireplace, or that he's replaced the dining room table with a pool table."

"I think that's the whole point of his having a new home," I said. "It's a chance to start over, to discover what he likes."

"Gary *knows* what he likes. He likes what *you* like. He *likes* the home you two built together in Pleasant Glen. This condo is lovely, but it's not a home, Julie, not without you in it. Oh, it has potential, but right now it's as nondescript as a hotel room. He can't do any business entertaining here, obviously. And it's so hard to develop a good working relationship at some impersonal restaurant." I got the hint. She thought I should be channeling all my time into organizing and hostessing these events for Gary – as if my time were any less valuable than his, or that of his executive secretary. I knew she was wrong, but I still felt guilty.

I told Helen that once Miss Irene's wedding was over, I would help Gary decorate. My real plan, however, was to send Emily. She had already spent a weekend with her dad picking out kitchen and bath supplies. They both told me they enjoyed the bonding experience, although Gary had drawn the line at buying lime green and pink bath towels.

Eventually my conversation with Helen turned to more social topics. Helen was getting to know the wives of Gary's colleagues, making all those social connections that I should have been taking care of. In fact, that afternoon the ladies were going to a sneak preview at an art gallery. As luck would have it, I was headed to the local art museum as well. It was the first time I would be meeting with the gallery director since Helen told me about their relationship. This meeting had the potential to be extremely awkward and uncomfortable. I was morbidly excited.

I was about to calm my nerves with a pint of cookie dough ice cream – making up for all the calories and flavor missing from my lunch – when my phone rang again.

"Hey, Jules." Gary's voice sent a shiver down my spine. He had a great phone voice – deep and smooth like a late-night radio host's – so it was the good kind of shiver. Except that he was my not-soon-enough ex-husband-to-be, so maybe it was a not-so-good kind of shiver.

"What wonderful things did Mom tell you about me today?" he asked. I could hear the smile in his voice. Gary had called me at least once every day when we first split up, asking me everything from what laundry soap I used to the best way to heat leftover pizza. I suspected those calls were suggested – if not outright scripted – by Helen to show how much Gary needed me. I came to dread those calls because they made me feel cranky. And guilty.

After a month, the calls tapered off and became less needy and more friendly. Now he only called once a week to touch base about Emily, our house in Pleasant Glen, and divorce proceedings – or *lack of* divorce proceedings. And sometimes he just called to chat – to share something that had happened at work. We were getting along better than we had in years, and I realized I liked him much better as a friend than I had as a spouse.

"What makes you think I've talked to your mom today?"

"I tried to call both of you and got a busy signal."

"That doesn't prove . . . ."

"It was after one-thirty, meaning Helen had moved on to social call number two. You know Helen's routine as well as I do. Nine to noon is reserved for business calls, one to four for social calls, and all calls are limited to thirty minutes. Miss Irene's circumstances have moved her up to call number one, putting you in the 'trust but verify' spot."

"They could set the atomic clock by your mom's schedule. She tried so hard to teach me time management skills, but I never quite caught on."

"You still managed okay. Always kept me in line and on schedule. I don't think I ever thanked you for that, by the way. I couldn't have done it . . . this promotion, my success . . . it's all because of you."

It's nice to be appreciated, even if it is long after the fact. All these compliments were going to my head. I tried to stay humble. "Eh, you're the numbers man. I just took care of the other stuff so you could concentrate on what you do best." *Just like Helen taught me*, I thought.

"I appreciate it, Jules. I probably didn't tell you that enough."

Gary sounded sincere, and I was more than a little flattered. But his sudden gratitude also made me suspicious. And *that* made me feel guilty.

"Now that we've established how wonderful I am, why did you really call, Gary?"

"I meant it all," Gary chuckled. "But you're right, there is something else. Did Mom say anything to you about Miss Irene's wedding?"

"No, she was pretty focused on your lack of decorating skills, and how empty your life is without me."

"I'm sorry about the hard sell, Jules. Mom's getting a little carried away with the whole matchmaker thing. I'm sure you realized running into you at The Bar during Miss Irene's party wasn't an accident."

"No one can feign a total lack of surprise quite like you."

"Mom means well. She really is worried about you. And me, of course. But these arranged coincidences are not fair to either of us. Which is why I called. Dad's not going to make it back for the wedding, so she asked me to be her escort. I wanted to run that by you first. I won't go if it will make you uncomfortable. I'll drive Mom back to Pleasant Glen, and then I can beg off with an emergency business meeting, if you'd like."

Gary was concerned about my comfort? How sweet. How chivalrous. How suspicious.

"No, that's alright. Your mom doesn't want to go alone, and Emily will be glad to see you. I'll be busy behind the scenes, anyway." That was all true, but shouldn't I be a little annoyed that Gary would be there? Or that Helen had tried to set us up yet again? Was Gary's attention making me soft? "All this . . . your concern is touching, but why now, Gary?" Why hadn't he been this concerned about my feelings while we were married?

"I've been thinking a lot since we split up, Jules. Even more now that Mom's here." Gary hesitated. "You know that Mom and Dad have a . . . unique relationship. Still, they make it work. Somehow. But lately, something's changed. Something's going on.

"Part of the reason I've been dragging my feet on the divorce is that I haven't been able to get a straight answer out of Dad about the mortgage on our house. I know I shouldn't have, but I let him take care of all the financing when we built it. He's the real estate agent, he had the contacts, so I figured why not go with the expert? He loaned me some money so we could make a bigger down payment and get a better interest rate, then offered to co-sign the loan so we could get an even better interest rate. Things were going good in Florida for them, so I figured they were looking for a safe investment, something to help defray taxes."

"But?"

"But now I've found out that Dad's name is on the deed and

he took out a second mortgage on the house. Short term, not a huge amount. Nothing illegal, just . . . questionable. It's making it more difficult to figure out our total assets. That's why this is taking so long. The thing is, he never told me. He never told Mom."

"Wow. That's . . . uh . . . huh." I wasn't looking to get a big divorce settlement. All I really wanted was a *quick* divorce settlement, so I could get on with my life with Joe. I got a sinking feeling in my stomach.

"And Jules, I don't think Dad ever intended to come back to Iowa with Mom for the wedding. Something's going on between them. But neither of them will tell me what."

That sinking feeling in my stomach sank lower. I had liked Richard – before I found out he was a serial philanderer. I liked Helen – despite the fact that she put up with Richard's cheating and thought I should stand by Gary. And I was starting to like Gary again – despite the fact that he had cheated on me. Seeing any marriage collapse, even one as dysfunctional as I thought Richard and Helen's was, made me sad.

"Oh, Gary. I'm so sorry. I . . . I'm sure it will all work out. Richard's an hon . . ." *honest* wasn't exactly the right word, ". . . a smart businessman. I'm sure there's an explanation. It will all work out." What can I say? When the going gets dismal, I become Olive Optimist. At least on the outside.

"I hope you're right, Jules. For Mom's sake. And for yours. I know you are . . . ready to move on. I'm sorry. For everything."

After that little bombshell, neither of us was much in the mood for small talk. Gary said he'd keep me posted, and I agreed not to grill Helen about it. Or hire a hit man to take out Richard. At least not until after we had settled the whole mortgage thing.

I had lost my appetite for ice cream and there wasn't enough time to go for a run to burn off my frustrations, so I decided to bury myself in work. I rolled up the sleeves on my Donna Karan collarless, black blazer, squeezed my feet into my leopard print loafers, slapped on some "Wine to Five" lipstick, and set off for the art museum.

Chapter 16

Despite taking the long way across town – and let's face it, there isn't really a "long way" to anywhere in Pleasant Glen – I arrived almost ten minutes early for my meeting, catching Mr. Cone's secretary off guard. I try to sell the fact that I am rarely on time and never early as part of my charm, but no one buys it. Especially not Jan . . . or Ann, or Fran, whatever the secretary's name is. I have trouble connecting a human name to her because she reminds me of the marble busts in the art gallery, with her porcelain complexion, ice-blue eyes, and white-blond hair. Her facial features barely move – whether because her bun is pulled too tightly or her botox was botched – making it difficult to gauge her emotions. I assume the worst, just to be safe.

Jan/Ann/Fran was working at her computer when I walked in. Her eyes flicked up, and I thought I saw one nostril flare slightly – her version of a sneer – as she greeted me.

"Mrs. Westbrook. Fashionably late as usua . . . oh." I saw her eyes flick to the time display at the bottom corner of her computer screen. The typing stopped. Her pencil-line eyebrows moved imperceptibly. "But you're . . . ." She looked up and actually made eye contact with me. The corners of her mouth quivered and tried to drop. She checked her watch and her cell phone and, finding I was still early, stared at me. Her eyes bulged slightly and her face took on a pink tinge as she struggled to frown.

"I'll let Mr. Cone know you're here." She tapped her headset. "Mr. Cone, Mrs. Westbrook is here to see you." She looked at her watch again. "Yes, I know." She tapped the face of her watch. "Yes, I know." She glared at me. I heard her grind her teeth. "Yes, I will." She tapped her headset again. "Mr. Cone will be with you in a moment. Please wait in his office." She returned to her typing.

"Don't. Touch. Anything," she said, without missing a keystroke.

The Pleasant Glen Art Museum was established in a turn-of-the-century brick mansion that had been donated to the city in the early 1970s. When a spacious, modern gallery area was added on in 1986, the museum offices and boardroom moved to the second floor of the house. Mr. Cone's office had once been the mansion's master suite and retained the high ceilings, tall windows, and handsome oak woodwork. His desk – a massive, wooden antique – faced the door, and two straight-backed chairs faced the desk.

Paintings and sculptures from Mr. Cone's personal collection were displayed throughout the room. I had seen them many times before, but – since I was always late – never had the time to examine them. Mr. Cone had worked at many world-class art museums throughout his career, including the Art Institute of Chicago. After he took early retirement and returned to Iowa to care for his aging father, Helen had been instrumental in bringing him to Pleasant Glen. He traveled frequently to lend his expertise and also used that clout to bring important works to our small museum. He respected the conservative morals of our community, yet each exhibit included two or three pieces that challenged those sensibilities, without giving offense.

I thought of that skill when I found myself drawn to one

collage in particular. It was nearly hidden behind the open door, but I realized it would have been directly in Mr. Cone's line of sight when he was at his desk and the door was closed. My first impression was of the colors, or lack of colors. It was a small piece, about the size of a large placemat, with scraps of black and white images and text obscured by an overlay of gray tissue paper. As I examined it more closely I could pick out advertisements for romantic getaways, sexy lingerie, jewelry, perfumes, and aphrodisiacs under the haze. In the bottom corner, mounted so it appeared to be bursting through the canvas, was a small, lavender box, a subtle contrast to the gray. The lid to the box was open, and it looked as if candy conversation hearts had spilled out. Instead of the usual "Be Mine" or "Kiss Me," these said "Honesty," "Laughter," "Kindness," "Attentive," and "Thoughtful."

I stepped back and let the images hide themselves again. All that gray depressed me. I wondered why Mr. Cone would hang this piece where he would have to see it every time he looked up from his work. When I stood next to his desk, however, my perception changed. Up close it had seemed like the gray was pouring down the canvas, filling the box. From this distance, the hearts were the first thing I noticed – brightly colored sparks suspended against an unobtrusive background.

I studied the collage, looking for the artist's signature. There, on the box, hidden amid intricate scrollwork, I found a name in quotation marks – "Christina."

"Ahh, Mrs. Westbrook. I'm sorry I kept you waiting. It's just that you are usually . . . ." Mr. Cone stopped, his hand on the doorknob, when he saw me looking at the collage. He gently took me by the elbow and led me to the guest chairs. "In fact, I can't recall that you've ever been . . . . Is everything alright? Is every*one* alright? Big George? Miss Irene?" He paused before sitting at his desk. "Helen?"

"I didn't realize what a calamity my being on time would cause," I said. "They're all fine. Miss Irene is . . ." I shook my head, "being Miss Irene. But the other two are fine. Big George scolded me this morning, and I spoke to Helen before I came here." I hesitated. "She sends you her regards." What harm could a little fib do?

Mr. Cone nodded and looked past me, toward the door. "Yes. Well. She's a considerate woman." He rearranged some papers on his desk. "I hope I didn't keep you waiting long. I was in the conservation area going over some details for the upcoming exhibit. Let me find a catalog for you. It might give you some ideas for the reception." He sifted through a file drawer. "I believe you know the basics. The artist has Iowa ties. For this particular series she has created pairs of watercolors juxtaposing farmscapes with seascapes." He handed me a slim catalog. "Quite fascinating, really. Rolling hills reimagined as ocean swells, tractors as ships, silos as lighthouses." As he spoke, he rocked slightly in his chair. I enjoyed listening to Mr. Cone talk about art, but it seemed like he was rambling.

"Some might call it 'sofa art' – relaxing, comforting works that would look right at home hanging over the sofa in the family living room. I'm sure it will be quite popular. A good back-to-school exhibit, I think. Lots of tie-ins for the children's art exploration classes." He hesitated, as if searching for something else to say, then settled for clearing his throat. "Do you have any questions?"

"I do. But, not about the exhibit."

He stopped rocking. After a long pause, he nodded his head.

"While I was waiting, I was admiring your collection. I found myself drawn to the collage by your door," I said.

"Yes." He steepled his fingers and resumed rocking. "It is thought provoking."

"Exactly! Up close I thought . . . but when viewed from this distance my perspective is completely different. Would you please tell me about it? I found the artist's name in quotation marks. Or I assume it was the artists name, anyway. That added to the mystery for me."

Mr. Cone hesitated. "Christina is a pseudonym. A 'nom de art,' if you will." He smiled. "A private joke between the artist and myself."

I sat quietly, thinking this over and hoping he would tell me more.

"Are you familiar with Andrew Wyeth's painting 'Christina's World'?" Mr. Cone gestured to a framed print hanging on the opposite side of the doorway from the collage.

I had been so focused on the unfamiliar work that I had ignored this iconic painting. Now as I looked at the two pieces, I imagined an arc stretching from the figure of the woman, up through the field to her house, across the doorway and down past the pastel hearts to the box. The placement seemed very deliberate and made me more curious.

"That painting always makes me feel a little sad," I admitted. Mr. Cone didn't reply. "The house seems so close, and so far away." The collage made me feel the same way, I thought. The sparks of color were hopeful, but the darkness was almost overpowering.

"That is a common response. However, I believe Wyeth

116

intended it to be uplifting. In interviews, Wyeth said he wanted to show Christina's strength – she was limited physically, but not spiritually. Despite her condition she was still able to move about the family farm." Mr. Cone came around to the front of his desk. "Despite the circumstances, the woman persevered." He glanced from one work of art to the other.

"I saw that same spark in . . . the artist of the collage. I told her so. She was hampered not by physical limitations, but by societal demands. By her own moral code." Mr. Cone rested his hand on the high back of the other visitor's chair and focused on the collage.

"There was something in her past. Something that shaped her, that she allowed to confine her. We are all a product of our past, are we not? Whether for good or for bad." He shrugged. "She never spoke of it but I could feel it in her artwork, I saw it in the way she responded to art. She bottled up her emotions, releasing them only through her creations. I felt privileged to witness this . . . vulnerability."

Mr. Cone nodded towards the Wyeth print. "I had the original here once, you know. My professional opinion on some minor restoration work was requested, but my health didn't permit travel . . . or so I claimed." He grinned. "This was a few years ago. I never really expected the museum to agree to send the painting . . . but for a few clandestine hours, 'Christina's World' and my world collided." He sat behind the desk again and resumed rocking.

"My artist friend had been having a particularly tough time. I thought seeing this painting might help her break free from her self-imposed restrictions. I hoped she would finally understand how much I cared for her.

"I asked her to come to the museum. I told her there had been a shipping error, and that I had something special to show her. Misleading, I know, but I wanted to surprise her. I opened a bottle of her favorite wine. Her favorite music was playing softly. The lights were low, a single spotlight trained on the painting. It was luminous. Breathtaking." I remembered how Helen had described that night in the conservation room.

"But she didn't . . . ." I said.

Mr. Cone shook his head sadly. "Perhaps I wanted too much, or pressed too hard. Perhaps there are some aspects of our history that can not be overcome."

"And then she . . . ."

"Yes. They moved to Florida. She delivered the collage personally, before they left. That was the last time I saw her . . . until Irene's party."

A clock in the gallery below us chimed five times. A soothingly modulated voice asked visitors to proceed to the exit.

"Life is short, Julie. Sometimes what we desire most is close at hand, if only we are willing to reach for it. I learned that from Miss Irene." He stood up, and I took that as my cue to leave.

"It is time for me to make my final rounds and check the doors," he said. "Look through the brochure. If you have questions about the featured exhibit, please don't hesitate to call. We will add a small exhibit before Christmas, and one after the first of the year. And after that . . . perhaps I will retire. Again."

I don't think Mr. Cone even noticed when I saw myself out. He was leaning against his desk, contemplating Helen's collage.

Chapter 17

I figured I'd had enough drama for one day, so I went back to my snug little apartment to open a bottle of wine, run a hot bubble bath, and listen to Joe's private recordings until the water turned cold. Or until I ran out of wine. And I had just bought a case of wine.

After making a few stops along the way, I pulled into the driveway shortly before six. J.J. and Big George pulled up right behind me in the shop truck – a gorgeous, cherry red, 1941 Chevy flatbed that I lusted after almost as much as I lusted after Paolo. The two vehicles couldn't have been any more different. Paolo was lean and sleek – the David Beckham of motorcycles– whereas the truck was big-boned and broad like Green Bay linebacker Clay Matthews. For all of Paolo's refined charm, there was something about all those curves and chrome on the truck that appealed to me in a "Dad bod" kind of way.

The engine was still running when Big George climbed down out of the truck. "Maybe you should clean up at Julie's first, Dad," J.J. called after him.

"I promised Miss Irene I'd be home by five. I'm late enough as it is! Evening, Julie," Big George said as he rushed by me. Even in the dusky twilight I could see that his short, white hair was sticking up wildly. His work shirt was covered in oil, grease and dirt, and there were black smudges across his chin and forehead. His right hand was wrapped in a wad of paper towels, and he limped slightly as he hurried up the sidewalk to the back door.

"Dad, I really think you . . . ." J.J. ran after his dad and motioned for me to follow him.

"What happened to him?" I asked as we chased Big George.

"Dad struggled with The Scout all afternoon. He got her put back together and then decided to go through everything again – but this time nothing went right. An oil hose worked loose and sprayed him. Then a bolt froze. He got a little too aggressive with the wrench and when the bolt gave he skinned up his knuckles."

"What about the limp?"

"He slipped in some brake fluid when he pushed back his rolling stool. Twisted his knee." J.J. shook his head. "If I believed all that hoodoo about The Scout talking to you nut jobs, I'd say she was telling him to keep his hands off."

"But she loves him!"

J.J. raised his eyebrows so high they nearly sailed off his head. That *did* sound a little crazy, even for me. "Well, you know what I mean."

"Unfortunately, yes. I do. I can't explain it Julie. I've never seen him have that much trouble with any engine – especially not The Scout. I've got to admit, it kinda creeped me out. You remember that Steven King book, *Christine*? Let's just say I didn't want to be in the shop alone with her."

That didn't sound at all like The Scout. Then again, she had been acting strange lately – more like a well-used 1941 motorcycle, and less like The Scout.

"George! What kept you so long? I've been worried sick!" Miss Irene shuffled out the back door. She stopped abruptly when Big George stepped into the light. "George!" she gasped. "Oh my lord! What happened to you?"

"Good evening, dear. Sorry to have kept you waiting" I thought Big George sounded like he was trying a little too hard to be casual. Apparently Miss Irene thought so, too. As he leaned over to kiss her cheek, she pulled away.

"Don't you 'good evening' me! You're a mess! And you're limping. Is that blood?" She took his bandaged hand in hers and gently removed the paper towels. "Good heavens! What have you done?"

"Oh, now, Irene. Just a few scraped up knuckles. They'll be right as rain in the morning."

"George Herbert Monroe! You promised me you'd stay in the office!" Miss Irene turned to J.J. "You! You promised to keep an eye on him!" I knew I should have gone straight up to my apartment, but it was too late now. Miss Irene had me in her sights as well. "And you! This is all because of that damn motorcycle, isn't it?" She glared angrily at each of us. "What were you thinking? Not a brain among the three of you! George! The doctor told you to take it easy."

"Now, Irene . . . ." George tried to calm her.

"You promised me you'd take it easy. You *promised*!"

"But . . . ."

"No buts! I can't do this! I won't sit back and watch you work yourself to death. I won't!" Miss Irene stomped toward the door. She nearly ran into Beatrice, who had come to see what all the yelling was about. Miss Irene spun on her heel to face Big George.

"You are moving back in with J.J. The wedding is off!"

Chapter 18

A quiet, persistent knocking woke me too early the next morning. I opened the door to find Beatrice wearing a velour, zip-front robe, her fluffy cloud of hair swaddled in toilet paper. She held her empty coffee mug in front of her with both hands, looking like some poor street urchin asking for alms.

"Mother threw out all her coffee, and I can't face another day of tea," Beatrice said pitifully. I sat her at my kitchen table and fired up the single-serve coffee maker. "I don't know what's gotten into her, Julie. This morning she went to early bird bingo at the American Legion. Can you imagine? My mother playing bingo? Voluntarily? Personally, I love bingo. Just not at the crack of dawn. But the last time I asked Mother to go to the bingo parlor, she said she'd play only if she could take a shot of tequila every time one of her numbers was called."

"Gives a whole new meaning to 'blackout bingo'," I quipped.

"Believe me, I checked her bag for a flask this morning before she left." Beatrice sipped her coffee, savoring every drop. She didn't speak again until the cup was empty. "Wouldn't a coffee delivery service be heavenly?" she asked in a dreamy voice.

"Would you like another cup?"

"Bless you, Julie! I thought about going to the bakery for coffee, but Mother has the car, and The Scout is out of commission, so I am homebound."

"The Scout? You mean . . . ."

"Oh yes! Big George taught all us kids to ride. He figured that was the only way to keep us safe. My brother Edward – second in line – was rather adventurous, and brother Albert – third – always got swept up in Edward's schemes."

"Did you ever . . . ."

"I never felt comfortable on The Scout. But the boys had a Honda minibike that was an awful lot of fun." Beatrice smiled. "I know Mother thinks I was the perfect child, but there were a lot of things she never knew about. Or at least I hope she didn't." I thought about all the things I hoped my mom never knew about, and all the things Emily had done that she didn't think I knew about. I snorted.

"Do you really think . . . ."

"Oh, no!" Beatrice laughed. "I'm sure Mother knew everything that went on. Or Big George did. He used to sit back in his chair, cross his arms over his chest and just look at us – completely neutral expression on his face. He didn't have to say a word. All that Catholic guilt would come bubbling to the surface and we'd confess to everything! Even the stuff we only *thought* about doing! After we'd cleansed our souls, he'd give us our penance and extract a vow to change our wicked ways. Between the six of us – seven with J.J. – we did a lot of stupid things. But we never did the same stupid thing twice. And we learned from each other's mistakes. Or learned how not to get caught!

"You know, Julie. I love my dad, but Big George was more of a father to me – to all of us. He was always there to interrogate boys on the first date. He greeted us from the porch swing if we missed curfew. He made sure a couple of my beaus never asked me out again, and dried my tears when my heart was broken."

"But Miss Irene said you were a Daddy's Girl – Frank's girl."

"I am," she nodded. "Daddy was the fun parent. He never had to discipline us. And he's charming – you've met him. After the divorce he dated these fancy, beautiful women, but he always called me his 'best girl.' Let's face it, Julie, I've worked my way up to plain looking. When I was a teen, I was homely as a mud duck. But Daddy made me feel like a princess.

"Daddy was a big kid. I felt like I had to look after him, like I looked after the others. And then, after the divorce, Daddy told me I had to look after Mother. I was so glad to have Big George around. I knew he'd take care of her. And me too, I guess.

"I don't know what's gotten into her, Julie! I mean, sure, there've been times I wished she wasn't so flamboyant, but . . . . I'll admit, I bought her the dress, the cardigan and the Swarovski crystal glasses chain, but it was all a joke. I never expected her to wear them. Well, except for the Swarovski crystal glasses chain. It's quite stunning. And practical.

"Then, last night, when she called off the wedding! What are we going to do, Julie?"

"Well, you'll never get the deposits back," I blurted. "Sorry. I reverted to professional party planner. I'm still in shock too."

Beatrice waved away my apology. "I said the same thing to Mother last night. It didn't bother her. Since it was mostly family that was invited, she's decided to host a family reunion instead. Us kids haven't all been back since Dad's third wedding. Maybe the fourth. The tension got a little high when Dad's bride-to-be was younger than his daughters-in-law. And I'll admit, I'm hoping she comes to her senses."

"It's not just the wedding, Beatrice. It's like she's trying to push Big George away entirely. And she just told me she couldn't imagine life without him."

We quietly finished our second cups of coffee, each lost in her own thoughts.

"You know, Big George taught me how to drive a stick shift in that old shop truck," Beatrice said.

"Ohhh!" I said enviously

"Isn't it gorgeous?" Beatrice giggled. "Big George would never let me drive it solo, though. He said a classy lady like me deserved a classy ride. I think it was because all the boys in town were crazy about it and he thought I'd attract the wrong kind of attention. My brothers used to beg him to let them borrow it for dates. Have you seen the size of that cab?" Beatrice wiggled her eyebrows. "Can you imagine what you could do in there at a drive-in?"

"Beatrice! That sounds like something Miss Irene would say!"

"Well, the apple doesn't fall far . . . . When we were little Mother would pile us all in the station wagon and we'd meet Big George and J.J. up at the Grandview Drive-In. We'd stretch out on piles of blankets on the flatbed, or in the back of the station wagon, and take in as much of the double feature as we could stay awake for.

"The first time I ever saw Mother and Big George kiss was at one of those movies. I remember it like it was yesterday. The younger kids were so excited to see 'The Shaggy Dog,' but they were out cold before 'South Pacific' even started."

"*Some Enchanted Evening*?" I asked.

"Yep." Beatrice smiled at the memory. "I was fifteen. I thought it was the most romantic thing I had ever seen. Big George and Mother were leaned up against the back of the cab. He had his arm around her – it was getting a little chilly – and her head was resting against his chest. She looked at him, he looked at her, and then . . . they kissed. It was just like in the movies. Slow, sweet, gentle, eyes closed, mouths closed," Beatrice raised an eyebrow. "The way first kisses were meant to be. Or so I thought.

"Then Edward and Albert woke up, noticed them, and started making retching noises. Mother blushed and scooted away, but Big George gave them one of his confessional looks and they straightened right up and focused on the screen again. Then he grinned and winked at me and I knew Mother was in good hands."

"Maybe she needs a reminder of those times," I said.

"Do you think it's that easy, Julie?"

"I don't know, Beatrice." I sighed. "I don't know."

Chapter 19

Miss Irene's wedding may have been put on hold – I refused to believe it was really canceled – but I still had a reception to plan for Vanessa's ex-husband and his new husband. I met the three of them at Vanessa's house for a tapas luncheon after Beatrice had been thoroughly caffeinated. It was another beautifully warm day, so we moved our après-lunch margaritas to the front porch. Between the pre-lunch margaritas and the during-lunch margaritas, we hadn't done much reception planning.

"What the heck is making that racket? Come on, moto-girl, name that tune!" Steve shouted. I had spent enough time around J.J. and Big George to become pretty good at identifying motorcycles from the sound of their engines and Steve took great delight in testing my ability. I didn't disillusion him by pointing out that most people in Pleasant Glen rode one of three brands – Harley, Honda or Yamaha – and that they don't sound anything alike.

I was sitting with my back to the street, but I closed my eyes to listen closer, playing along. The bike slowed then accelerated – rounding a corner, I guessed. The exhaust was definitely attention getting. Demanding, actually. The engine kept an even tempo – not a Harley. The pitch was too low to be a Honda and too mellow to be a Yamaha. It was a deep, rumbly purr, like a contented lion.

As the bike drew closer, the sound of the wheels on the brick streets added a fluttering counterpoint. The rider downshifted, and the bike responded with a smooth *hmmm.* They glided to a crawl and finally stopped in front of the house. The rider let the engine idle a moment, and I detected a subtle note of familiarity just before he killed the engine.

Ciao, bella.

"Paolo." I whispered, slowly opening my eyes.

"What? I think we stumped you, moto-girl," Steve crowed.

Vanessa, who was sitting opposite me, was on her feet and at the top of the stairs before I could turn around. "Is that our J.J.?"

Our J.J.? Since when was he *our* J.J.? And why would *our* J.J. be riding the Moto Guzzi he *wouldn't let me ride*? Vanessa bit her bottom lip and wiggled her fingers at the driver in a flirty wave, then rushed down the steps.

"Our" J.J. doesn't wear a sporty, leather racing jacket like that, I thought.

Steve squirmed in his seat and squinted to get a better look. "I don't like this."

Vanessa was standing next to the rider now. She rocked on her toes and clasped her hands behind her. The rider reached up to take off his helmet. *"Our" J.J. doesn't wear a full-face helmet like that.*

Vanessa shifted her weight to one side, changing position just enough to completely block my view of the rider's face. She tilted her chin down slightly. Her shoulders shook as she giggled. Was she flirting with him?

"I don't like this one bit!" Steve said.

The rider handed Vanessa his helmet, then pulled a pair of wraparound sunglasses from a pocket inside his jacket.

"Our" J.J. doesn't wear wrap-around sunglasses.

Steve started to get up off the swing. "What does she think she's . . . ." Michael gently restrained him.

Vanessa swung her leg over the bike and wrapped her arms much too tightly around the driver. He leaned to the side opposite of us and, I assumed, showed her where to put her feet. Then, still looking away from us, he repositioned her arms – pulling her even closer. She leaned against his back. He flicked the starter and goosed the throttle. She rested her head on his shoulders. He put the motorcycle in gear. They pulled away with a growl, although I wasn't sure if that was from the motorcycle or from Steve.

"Our" J.J. wouldn't . . . . Would he?

"Why, I've got half a mind to . . . ."

"Steve, dear, relax. She's a grown woman."

I wished Michael hadn't interrupted Steve, because I was pretty sure I had the other "half a mind to . . . ." Although to *what*, I wasn't sure.

"What the hell? Are you just going to sit here and let her ride off with that hoodlum? Do something, Michael!"

"What do you want me to do, Steve, darling? She's a grown woman."

"She didn't ask permission."

"Grown woman."

"She didn't tell us where they were going, when they'd be back . . . . She didn't even introduce him to you!"

"That's because I'm her ex-husband, not her father."

"And I'm her ex-husband's new husband. That counts for *some*thing. That *should* count for something!"

"Steve, calm down. Drink your margarita."

"Drink my margarita? Really, Michael? Your ex-wife, my

ex-wife-in-law rides off on the mechanical embodiment of testosterone, and you want me to calm down and drink my margarita? Tequila is not going to solve this, Michael. Tequila is not going to help me calm down!"

"I know where her emergency stash of chocolate is," I said.

Steve looked at me, crossed his arms over his chest and threw himself back in the swing. "It better be Godiva."

The next thirty minutes felt like an eternity. While we waited – on the porch – for Vanessa and J.J. to return, we continued planning the reception. Vanessa's absence and our obsession with it – as well as my tequila headache – sucked the fun right out of planning.

Steve and Michael were simultaneously thrilled and freaked out that Vanessa's parents wanted to throw them a party. We decided to use the generic term "party" instead of "belated wedding reception" to downplay the awkwardness of the situation. Vanessa's parents had been severely ostracized when word got out about Vanessa sleeping with my husband. Gary's infidelity – like that of his father – was conveniently overlooked. But now, having a gay ex-son-in-law had made Betty and Walter celebrities at the senior center and redeemed their reputations, along with Vanessa's. Michael and Steve looked at it as a "Gay Outreach" opportunity. A couple of Betty and Walter's friends had already asked them for advice on how best to support children and grandchildren who were coming out.

We were discussing centerpieces when Steve's concentration shattered. "Who was that man? How does she even know such a hoodlum?"

"J.J.'s my . . . ." I started to explain.

"Bah! You and your rock and roll boyfriend! You and your

freaky, moto-girl hoo-doo!"

"No, he's Miss Irene's . . . ."

"Oh, dear god! The pole dancer is involved?"

"Julie. Not helping," Michael muttered.

"He's Big George's son."

"Great! His dad's the Viagra poster boy!"

"Not helping."

"It's not like that. Big George never took . . . ."

"Even worse!"

"Not. Helping."

"No, Michael. She's not helping. And neither are you! How can you be so calm about this? Your ex-wife just rode off with the leather-clad son of a libidinous 90-year-old on a motorcycle that is so sexy the exhaust tests positive for steroids, and you're not the least bit upset?"

"Vanessa is a smart woman, Steve. Except for that unfortunate encounter with Gary, she has never been sexually irresponsible. And heaven knows, she had plenty of reason to be sexually irresponsible."

"Gary *is* a good looking man," Steve conceded.

"I mean, when we were married . . . but we weren't . . . well, you know . . . sexually compatible. From the little I know of him, J.J. is a good man."

"He's a devoted single father and a responsible son," I added.

"And well, even if he isn't, doesn't she deserve a little . . . fun?" Michael concluded.

"Not. Helping." I said.

"Whose side are you on?" Steve asked me.

"Side? I'm not on *anyone's* side. There are no sides. They are both responsible adults who . . . ."

"Who have been effectively celibate for how long? And they are on the sexiest motorcycle I have ever seen! It's a phallus on wheels! If Dwayne 'The Rock' Johnson was a motorcycle, he still wouldn't be half as sexy as that motorcycle. And heaven knows I would love to have me a piece of 'The Rock'!

"How can you be so heartless, Michael? Don't you feel even the least bit guilty? Because I sure as hell do!"

Michael sighed wearily. "I love Van. I always have and I always will. It's true, Julie. I want Van to be happy. Not just 'happy'," he said, making air quotes, "but insanely happy, the way you make me, Steve." He reached out to hold Steve's hand. "I want *this* kind of happiness for her. She deserves that.

"I have spent my entire life feeling guilty. If there's one thing I've learned from all that guilt and misery, it's that you have to take responsibility for your own happiness. No one else can make you happy, and you can't make anyone else happy. Vanessa has to find happiness for herself. The only way she can do that is to get out there and . . . turn over a few 'Rocks'."

Steve had tears in his eyes, and so did I. Damn it. Now that Michael and Vanessa were divorced, I liked him a lot better.

"And that's why I love you, you terrible, heartless, incurable romantic!" Steve hugged Michael. "But I'm still going to give her so much shit when she gets back."

"You and me both, sister. You and me both!" Michael laughed.

Chapter 20

We were still sitting on the porch when Vanessa and J.J. returned. The Guzzi glided up to the curb and Vanessa gave J.J. one last squeeze before dismounting. She took the helmet off and, with one graceful shake of her head, her wavy, red hair returned to full-bodied perfection. I have never hated her as much as I did at that moment. I get helmet hair from just looking at helmets. As she handed the helmet back, she leaned in and gave J.J. a kiss on the cheek. J.J. sat there, looking a little dazed as she sauntered back to the porch. I was certain there was a little more hip swing to her walk than usual. J.J. smiled, then looked up at us and waved before putting the helmet on and leaving.

Once she heard the motorcycle pull away, Vanessa sprinted up the stairs.

"J.J. said to tell you he's talked with Beatrice and everything's under control," she said, breathlessly. Then she whispered "My room. Now!" before hurrying in to the house.

"Was her shirt . . . ." I started to ask before I considered whether I should be asking it.

"On inside out?" Michael said. "And did she . . . ."

"Have a hickey?" Steve added.

I realized too late that I had opened a can of worms. "I'm going to . . . um . . . ." I said, easing toward the door. I assumed Vanessa's whispered message to meet her had something to do with her disheveled appearance.

"Oh, no! You're not talking girl talk without me!" Steve jumped up and followed me, with Michael close behind. We found Vanessa standing at the foot of her bed, taking her shirt off. When she realized she had an audience, she held it up in front of her, modestly.

"Oh, please! There's nothin' there she doesn't have, nothin' Michael hasn't already seen, and nothin' that interests me," Steve said, making himself comfortable on her bed. "What the hell? You're gone for an hour, and you come back with a hickey? How did you even have enough time to get a hickey? And what kind of hoodlum gives a girl a hickey at our age? For heaven's sake, I thought you two said this guy was responsible!"

"No! It's not what you . . . J.J. didn't . . . ." Vanessa sputtered.

"Holy shit! It was someone else? I don't know if I should applaud or be shocked!" Steve said.

"No! No. It's not a hickey! J.J. was a perfect gentleman! It was me . . . er, a bug . . . I mean . . . ." Vanessa sighed and lowered her shirt. Several angry, red, scratch marks ran down her neck and across her chest, disappearing beneath her bra.

"Oh my god, Van! What happened?" I asked.

"Michael, would you please get me a cold, wet washcloth and the allergy stuff? It's all still in the same place in the medicine cabinet." She sighed again. "I would ask you guys to leave, but I know you'll just listen at the door, anyway."

Steve looked a little hurt. "Well, duh!"

"To begin with, J.J. stopped by to give you Beatrice's message, Julie. They've been trying to call you, but you weren't answering your cell phone." A quick check showed that I had several missed calls, and that my ringer was off. Again.

"I asked him to give me a ride. He said that motorcycle wasn't really built for two. I said I didn't care, I just needed to get away for a little while." Vanessa's eyes filled with tears. She took the washcloth Michael handed her and pressed it to her face before moving it to the scratches. "I guess I started to cry then, too. J.J. didn't say anything, just handed me the helmet and helped me climb on. Next thing I knew, we were at Oaks Landing."

The first time I took The Scout for a real ride, I had gone to that same little park along the river. The road there didn't get much traffic, and it was smooth, with wide, gentle curves. The scenery was iconic Iowa – rolling fields broken up here and there by trees or farmsteads.

"We parked near the boat landing and walked along the river, past the picnic area. Finally he asked if I wanted to talk about it. No pressure, no judgment, just 'Want to talk about it?'" Vanessa sank down on the end of the bed. "I love you guys, and I'm so happy you found each other. But all this reception planning is . . . ."

"Oh, honey! We don't have to . . . ." Steve and Michael both moved to comfort her, but she held up her hand to stop them.

"No! You two love each other, and that is something to celebrate! It's just, sometimes I get a little jealous. And then I feel guilty because you've both been so sweet. Especially you, Steve."

"Best ex-husband-in-law you'll ever have."

"But the scratches, Van. What happened?" I asked.

"J.J. said he understood how I felt. He said that he loved Big George and Miss Irene, but that all the wedding planning had been wearing on him. He feels guilty now that they've put things on hold. I hadn't realized what a sweet guy he is, Jules. I mean, he always seemed to be wound so tight, what with the business and Trey and Big George."

"The scratches, Van."

"Well, we walked along the edge of the woods by the shelters and . . . I managed to stir up a swarm of those nasty orange Asian Lady Beetles – the ones that look like Ladybugs but aren't?"

"Oh, Van! You poor thing!" I knew Vanessa had developed an irrational fear of Asian Lady Beetles after Phil Thompson threatened to put one up her nose in third grade.

"Yeah, well, those little bastards were all over me! I freaked out, completely froze! I couldn't even swat them away. J.J. gently brushed them out of my hair, off my . . . everything. The whole time he was gently talking to me, trying to calm me down.

"Then he put his hands on my waist and pulled me a little closer. He looked me in the eyes and asked if I was alright. All I could think about was how much I wanted to kiss him, and I leaned forward and he leaned forward and I think he was about to kiss me when I felt a little tickle by my collar . . . . So I stopped. And then J.J. stopped. But the tickling didn't stop. It moved down my chest. And so I shimmied a little. And J.J. backed up a little. And the tickle kept moving lower. And I froze again. And J.J. asked if I was okay. And I told him I didn't think I was alone in my bra.

"J.J. made kind of a choking sound, but he didn't laugh . . . like you assholes!" It was true. Steve and Michael weren't laughing out loud, but their shoulders were shaking and they had tears running down their faces from trying to hold it in.

"He said 'I'm going to let you take care of that.' Then he took his jacket off and held it up to shield me, just in case any boaters came back. I ripped my shirt off and waved it around like a crazy woman, swatting and scratching and cussing the whole time.

"J.J. was such a gentleman. When I finally got things . . . sorted out, I lowered his jacket, and he even had his eyes closed! Which, you know, could have been a little offensive, but . . . he was so sweet. Anyway, I thanked him and apologized for all the fuss. I figured I had blown any chance I had with him. I mean, I try not to go full-on crazy until at least the third date.

"But he got this little twinkle in his eye – just like Miss Irene and Big George do – and he said when you ride a motorcycle you get used to having bugs in places they're not supposed to be. 'This isn't the first time a bug has gotten to second base before me,' he said. Then he said he had to get back to work."

Vanessa sighed and got a faraway look on her face. "Then he asked me out for dinner tonight."

"See? I told you two she'd be fine," Steve said. Michael rolled his eyes. "There's absolutely nothing to worry about!"

Vanessa giggled. "He's picking me up at six. He said we'd take the shop truck."

I thought there was plenty to worry about.

Chapter 21

As much as I wanted to see Steve's reaction to the seductively roomy shop truck, and as much as I wondered *what* Beatrice had under control, I had to leave. Joe was home for the weekend – wedding/reunion included – but he had a session scheduled at his home studio, so our time together was limited. Naturally, I was running late and Joe's flight arrived in Des Moines early.

Joe lives on the family farm in a rural no-man's-land most easily referred to as "north-east of Des Moines." His is one of a patchwork of farms encompassing three small towns that have faded to blips on the official Iowa DOT map. Between them they share one consolidated school district, two combination gas station/mini marts, three bars and four churches. Here and there suburbia had stretched out a tentacle and, finding lower property taxes, established outposts. Settlers, traveling by SUV wagon train, traversed the rolling blacktop and forded aerated ponds to homestead amongst the ornamental grasses, far beyond the reach of free pizza delivery.

I passed the wrought-iron gates and manicured lawns of Prairie's Edge Estates and took the next gravel road on my left. A faded sign cautioned that this road became a level "B" maintenance dirt road ahead. The sign showing a "T" intersection this side of the dirt road had disappeared years ago. I turned onto the paved intersecting road, passed a farm house on the left and pulled into the drive across from it. Joe's white, two-story farmhouse looked out over a football-field-sized lawn dotted with hosta-ringed trees, peony bushes and clumps of tiger lilies. An L-shaped cornfield wrapped round the big, red, barn-turned-recording studio across the driveway from the house.

Joe was on the porch, talking with Effie and Donald Steen, his neighbors from across the road. Their son Mike and his wife have a house on the back lot of Prairie's Edge Estates. Mike's house can be reached from the subdivision's gated front entrance – his wife's preference – or from a field road on his parent's farm – Mike's preference. Together, Mike and Donald rent farmland from Joe and look after his place when he's gone. Effie looks after Joe when he's home. They had brought Joe a bucket full of tomatoes, and grocery sacks filled with what everyone hoped would be the last harvest of green peppers and zucchini.

Joe and I stayed outside after they left, listening to the lowing and shuffling of cattle at the Steen's feedlot and the drying corn stalks rattling in the breeze. Bullet, a shaggy, mostly border collie farm mutt with mismatched eyes, begged Joe to play fetch. The dog had been fast as a speeding bullet when he was a puppy, Joe said, but his ability to mooch treats had left him with more of a cannon ball shape. The barn cats lounged on the porch, staying just out of reach and feigning disinterest until I ignored them. When Joe's arm tired from throwing the soggy tennis ball for "Bully," and the cats had all had their ears scratched, Joe and I went inside to start dinner.

The kitchen was my second favorite room in Joe's house. Sophia had insisted he remodel it for entertaining purposes, and while she and I did not see eye to eye on most things, I had to admit it was gorgeous. Oak cabinets, black quartz countertop and a white, apron-front farmhouse sink – pardon me while I swoon – made the room warm and homey without being kitschy.

Joe stood between the island and the stove, where he could do prep work and cook. I sat on the opposite side of the island, where I could drink wine. I watched appreciatively while he chopped the vegetables as smoothly as he played the piano. I watched even more appreciatively when he turned to the stove. Joe looked just as good in a faded pair of jeans as he did in a designer suit. Or in nothing at all.

"I could help, you know," I said, despite the fact that I was enjoying not helping.

"You *are* helping," Joe replied. "You opened the wine."

"No, I'm *sampling* the wine. You *opened* the wine. I would still be pulling on the cork if you hadn't rescued me. Or I'd be covered in wine. I've never been much good with a waiter's corkscrew."

"You have to ease the cork out. Slow and steady. Gentle motions." Joe demonstrated by deftly – and seductively – peeling a blanched tomato. "You know what they say about a '*slow hand*,' and an '*easy touch*'," he said, grinning suggestively.

"The Pointer Sisters were right, you know."

"I was thinking more along the lines of Del Reeves, but whatever it takes." Joe shrugged and went back to his cooking.

"Is there anything sexier than a man who can cook?" I mused aloud.

"A man who does dishes?"

"Ooooh. You got me there!" I sighed dramatically. "Truly, the way to a woman's heart is through mastery of the domestic arts."

"I thought you were just sampling the wine. Maybe I should cut you off." Joe glanced over his shoulder. "I wouldn't want to be accused of taking advantage of you."

"Not a chance! This is my first glass." At least I thought it was. The wine nearly sloshed over the side of the glass as I pulled it across the counter, despite my slow but steady drinking.

"I take it Barry wasn't much help in the kitchen?" Joe asked.

"Not hardly." Just the thought of Barry – I mean Gary – lending a hand made me laugh.

"That's not . . . ." A sudden flare of sizzling turned Joe's attention back to the sauté pan before he could finish his sentence. Joe and I rarely talked about our previous relationships. Maybe it wasn't the healthiest way to deal with things, but I figured there was no point in picking at a scab. Still, I realized my comment and delivery may have sounded a little more bitchy than I intended.

"I mean, he *was*. In the beginning. Sort of. As time went on I saw it as part of my job. You know, the whole work-from-home thing."

Joe nodded, but said nothing. I thought about my talk with Mary. There were things – important things – Joe and I needed to discuss. The wine had given me just enough courage to start that discussion.

"I'm still trying to figure out what my role is now. With you." I took a deep breath and forged ahead. "Sometimes I'm not sure what I bring to this relationship." Joe stopped chopping vegetables, looked up at me and tilted his head questioningly. "I mean, with Gary, my job was to make sure his job went smoothly. I cooked, I cleaned, I entertained, I handled the dry cleaning. With you . . . I sit and drink wine while you work."

"You keep Sophia and Bob from killing each other," Joe said, grinning.

"True. That is a little more hazardous than dropping off dry cleaning. But on the other hand, Sophia and Bob wouldn't be thrown together so often if not for me, either. So that one doesn't really count. You would – you do – get along perfectly well without me. But I do like being able to help out. I just . . . need you to need me, I guess."

"And I '*want you to want me.*' I forgot how much you like Cheap Trick."

"Great. Now I'll have that song stuck in my head all night. And I never get the line after '*didn't I see you crying*' right."

"That's okay. I've heard that no one – and I mean *no one* – does." While I suspected that was true, it didn't make me feel any better. In fact, Joe's insider knowledge made me feel worse. It was just another example of how much of his life was foreign to me.

"I want you, Julie. I need you." Joe put down his knife, took the wine glass from me and finished it. "This is the first time in a long time I've been able to separate my work life from my private life. Ex number one was a musician. We were the record label's golden couple. Ex number two was famous for being famous. We were the tabloid's golden couple. Sophia and I had a business relationship long before it became personal." He shook his head. "Even then it was more . . . a matter of convenience. Sophia enjoys the finer things in life – whether they're provided by me or one of her millionaires. I enjoyed having an attractive companion without having to work at it. I'm not proud of that, but it's true. If Sophia had to choose between me and work, she'd pick work. That's why the wi-fi signal is weak in the bedroom. I got tired of being upstaged by her iPad.

"But with you, I can . . . make spaghetti sauce, or play with Bully and the cats, or sit in with Mary and the Shepherds. When the crowds are heading for the exits, I know that you'll be backstage waiting for me. For *me* – Joe Davenport the *man*, not Joe Davenport the *musician*. All that time we were apart, I never stopped thinking of you.

"So, yeah. I need you, Julie. *'And I want you for all time'*."

Joe knew how "Wichita Lineman" affected me. He had sung it to me once over the phone when he was in Oklahoma, half-way through a two-week tour. I missed him so badly I nearly jumped in the car right then, although by the time I got to Norman he would have been boarding a flight in Portland. I had cried that night, and I was teary eyed again.

"And *this* is *your* wine glass," Joe said, reaching for something on the counter beyond my left elbow. There sat my empty glass, hidden in plain sight. I took comfort in the fact that while I may be blind, at least I wasn't becoming a lightweight drunk. Joe slid the glass over and re-filled both of our glasses.

"Why didn't you tell me that before?" I asked, trying to mask my chagrin with irritation.

"What? And miss that look on you face? You're pretty cute when you're indignant."

"And you're lucky you can cook."

Joe laughed and turned back to the stove. "I knew it all along, you just want to keep me barefoot, pregnant and in the kitchen."

"Well, now. That's certainly something to consider."

"Nuh-uh. Not until you *'put a ring on it'*." Joe waved his hand at me and wiggled his hips, all without interrupting his stirring. His moves would have made Beyoncé proud.

I sang the "Oh *oh oh*" part of the song – or tried to – hoping to get Joe to dance a little longer. And to buy time. Of all the things we had *not* talked about, getting married and starting a family were perhaps the biggest omissions.

The getting married part was a given, I figured. Probably. Someday. After my divorce came through, of course. But there was no need to rush into anything.

The starting a family part? It was still possible, I guess. Probably. After all, I was 50. Almost 51. Time was definitely not on our side. But having a baby didn't seem like something we should rush into.

Joe was still sautéing and singing. And dancing. *Oh oh oh*, those hips. *Oh, oh, oh*, that man.

"Have you ever thought about having kids?" I asked. "With me?"

Joe stopped stirring. He stopped moving. He may have even stopped breathing, for all I know. I certainly had. He turned around slowly, and I watched as a range of emotions flashed across his face.

Surprise: "Are you . . . ?" His eyes opened wide.

Concern: "Should you . . . ." He pointed at the wine.

Confusion: "But we . . . ?" He swayed slightly, then steadied himself on the island. Joe and I always practiced safe sex. Well, almost always.

Remembrance: "There was that weekend in New York. . . . ." Joe got a faraway look in his eyes. Between our schedules we hadn't been together in the same place at the same time to have sex very often.

Recognition: "Or Chicago that one time . . . or two . . . ." We were definitely a quality, not quantity kind of couple. And the quality was outstanding.

Understanding: "So we could have . . . ." Joe's grin faded and his eyes came back into focus.

I didn't know if the next emotion would be terror or joy, and I wasn't sure I wanted to know.

"No! No, I'm not!" I said, putting an end to the guessing game. "I just realized we had never talked about it. I mean, it is still theoretically possible. You read about celebrities having babies in their fifties. They have movies about it on Lifetime." I was rambling, and I knew it. "So . . . ."

Joe nodded his head thoughtfully. He came around to my side of the island and sat on the barstool next to mine.

"I have thought about it, Julie, Not lately. Well, not as *much* lately." He paused. "Back when . . . well, the first time around, when we were younger . . . . Yeah, I thought about it. Even after you were married to Barry and I was married . . . and married again . . . . Whenever I thought about having a family, it was with you. I love you, Julie. I love Emily. If we have . . . I'll love him, too."

"Or her," I said.

"Or her," Joe laughed.

"Or them."

"I just got you back, Julie." Joe kissed my forehead. "One theoretical baby at a time, please."

"Fair enough." I took another sip of wine.

"What about you? What do you want?"

"I want you, Joe Davenport." I slipped off my chair, wrapped my arms around him and kissed him. "I think I've made that abundantly clear."

"Don't try to change the subject," Joe said, unwrapping himself from my embrace.

"Technically, the two subjects are related."

Joe held my arms at my sides. "Answer the question, sweetheart. Please?"

"You would make a wonderful father, Joe. And I would love to share that bond with you . . . . But I'm not sure I could handle those late nights any more."

"Ahh, the dreaded two a.m. feedings?"

"Not just them. It's the slumber parties. The junior high dances. After Prom parties. Ear aches, broken hearts, dates."

Joe pulled me back to him. "As appealing as you make that all sound, I'm not sure I could survive it, either. But there's nothing to keep us from trying, right?"

"Nothing I can think of." Of course, when we were alone and Joe was holding me close, I couldn't think of *anything* besides how much I wanted to make love to him.

"And this sauce is much better after it has rested a while," he said.

"You're not just trying to get out of doing the dishes, are you?"

"Not a chance." Joe tilted my chin up and kissed me gently. "Washing dishes is my *second* favorite activity."

"I love it when you talk domestic to me." I returned his kiss a little less gently.

"In that case, have I ever told you about my laundry skills? I can fold fitted sheets." I moaned softly – although that may have been in response to the way Joe's body pressed against mine and not his impressive folding abilities.

"I almost forgot how talented you are, Joe Davenport."

"I could demonstrate for you. Maybe even show you how I make the bed, complete with hospital corners."

"Wouldn't we need to *unmake* the bed before you could show

me how you make it?"

"You're in luck." Joe chuckled, low and sexy. "That's my *most* favorite activity."

That night Joe reminded me of his many talents – including all my favorites.

Chapter 22

I felt Joe's absence long before the squeak of the screen door woke me. It didn't matter if he was halfway across the country or out in the yard, that dull, empty ache was just as intense. I lay in bed a moment longer, calming my fears, before pulling the quilt around my shoulders and going to the window to look for him.

It had turned cold overnight. Ghostly strands of fog hovered in low spots out in the fields. Joe was heading across the drive to the barn which housed his studio. Bully and the cats danced around his ankles, slowing his progress. Joe swung open the wide door to the storage room at the near end and went inside. The animals sat on the gravel, watching and waiting, until he reappeared carrying dented tin pans. Joe set out food and water, and redirected one cat who tried to steal Bully's breakfast. Then he disappeared back into the storage room.

The cats were cleaning their faces and Bully was pacing anxiously when Joe emerged again, pushing a motorcycle. From my second-story perch, it appeared to be a mass of chrome pipes clustered between two wheels, topped by a slim, black gas tank. The cats stopped grooming and skittered away. Bully slunk toward the house, tail between his legs and head low.

I watched as Joe went through his pre-ride list – checking the oil, tires, and lights – his movements measured and deliberate. He carefully filled the gas tank, then reset the fuel cap and wiped away errant traces of gas. He returned the can to the garage and emerged wearing a hip-length, leather jacket, and an open-faced helmet.

I thought the process of starting The Scout was long and involved, but it was nothing compared to Joe's routine. He set and adjusted controls, valves and levers before mounting the bike. Then he checked everything one last time before rising out of the seat for the kick start. He bobbed smoothly through the motions – short stroke, pause, long stroke. The engine roared to life.

Joe settled onto the seat, leaving one hand on the handlebars to work the throttle. He cocked his head and listened. A few more adjustments, subtle changes, and the engine settled into a rhythm. Knowing that Joe thought in music rather than words, I closed my eyes and tried to hear what he heard, to think like he thought. I called on all my "moto-girl hoodoo," as Steve called it, to parse the Vincent's voice. I listened for the harmony created between the engine and the exhaust. The Scout had a smooth, sultry sound that wrapped around me. Joe's Vincent sounded melancholy, with a slightly uneven, shuffling rhythm that unsettled me.

Joe eased the bike into gear and carefully started down the driveway. He swung wide, making a graceful swoop, then smoothly accelerated out onto the county road. I stood at the window until the sound of the engine was swallowed by the mist.

Joe still hadn't returned by the time I showered and dressed. I filled two travel mugs with coffee and went outside to sit on the porch swing. Bully lay at the top of the stairs, his head hanging over the edge, watching the road. I had finished my mug and started to drink Joe's when Bully sat up and looked at me. He cocked his head, hitting me with the full guilt-inducing force of his mis-matched, puppy dog eyes.

"I swear, I'll refill it before he . . . ." Bully turned his back to me, apparently tired of my excuses. Then I heard it too, the low growl of Joe's motorcycle, calling out across the fields. Bully glanced over his shoulder and huffed. I wondered how many treats it would take to get back in his good graces.

Joe turned up the driveway and coasted past the house, gravel popping under his wheels. He stopped near the barn, took off his helmet and sat for a moment as the motorcycle's song echoed between the outbuildings. Finally he shook his head, set the bike on its kickstand, and went into the barn. I was waiting, coffee in hand, when he emerged with a towel.

"I could get used to this," he said, taking the mug and lifting it to his lips. "It's nearly empty."

"You were gone a long time."

"Maybe you were up too early." He laughed and pulled me close. "I figured you'd sleep in this morning. It was kind of a late night."

"The bed was lonely without you."

"Good to know." Joe kissed me once more before gently steering me towards the house. "I need to clean up here . . . then I'll be in to keep you company."

"I'll wait." I turned back and sat on a knee-high, stone wall. Once upon a time it had been the foundation of another barn. Now it kept cars from parking in the field and gave the cats a place to sun themselves.

Joe looked at me a moment, then shrugged. "Suit yourself." He moved to the motorcycle and began wiping away dust and bugs, and checking hoses and seals. He worked carefully, glancing up at me occasionally, but not speaking until he'd gone over everything twice.

"Engine's too warm to finish," he said at last. He sat next to me and we listened to the tick of the cooling metal. Joe took another drink of coffee, emptying the mug. "Any chance I could get a refill?"

"Any chance you're going to tell me about your motorcycle?"

"Good thing I brought my own thermos." He kissed my cheek, then walked to the barn. There went my only bargaining chip. When he returned, he swung the thermos by the handle, taunting me.

"Any chance I can buy you off?" he asked, pouring coffee into the thermos cap for me.

"What do you think?"

Joe blew the steam from his mug and took a drink. "What do you want to know?"

"Why didn't you tell me?"

"I didn't think it was important," he shrugged. "Why does it matter?"

Why *did* it matter to me? I thought for a moment before answering.

"It's not so much the *having* a motorcycle, as the *not telling* me about it." I cringed. *Insecure much?* Well, yes. Apparently. "It's just, there's so much I still don't know about you. When we're together, none of that matters because I'm just so happy to be with you. But when we're apart . . . I think about it. A lot. And lately we've been apart a lot."

Joe nodded, but didn't say anything. I rushed to fill the silence.

"So when Big George had his episode and was in the hospital

and he started singing that song about the Vincent Black Lightening, I asked J.J. what a Vincent was and . . . ."

"J.J.'s lucky he's a good mechanic," Joe interrupted.

"*We're* lucky he's a good mechanic."

Joe rolled his eyes. "There are better."

"Yeah, but Big George doesn't work on Vincents."

"He would for you." Joe grinned and bumped my shoulder with his.

"Maybe. Maybe not. I don't think Miss Irene wants him around *any* motorcycle right now. I think she's afraid he's going to work himself to death."

"Is that why she called off the wedding?"

It was my turn to shrug. "Maybe. "

"But he's 'the motorcycle whisperer'."

"You didn't see him the other night," I shook my head. "He was a mess – oil everywhere, bloody knuckles. He's been over and over The Scout and he can't figure out what's wrong. The harder he tries, the worse it gets."

Joe folded and refolded the towel. "Some things have unexpected consequences. Like this motorcycle." He stood up. "How much did J.J. tell you?"

"Nothing, really. He seemed surprised that I didn't know about your Vincent."

"*My* Vincent? I just pay the bills." Joe put his hands on his hips and looked the motorcycle over, wheel to wheel. "It's more J.J.'s Vincent than mine. Or Rollie's." He shook his head. "My name's on the title. That's about all."

Joe squatted down and started wiping the engine. He looked at me over the seat. "What do you think of it?"

"It's . . . impressive. But it's a little . . . off-putting." It was hard to explain. This motorcycle didn't have the low-slung profile of a cruiser like The Scout, or the pulse-racing angularity of the Moto Guzzi. "It's all those pipes and hoses snaking out from the engine. It's like it's been turned inside out." I shuddered.

"Vincents have been called the 'plumber's nightmare'."

"I can see why. The sound is . . . something else, too. I mean, it sounds good, but . . . kinda, melancholy."

"J.J. tuned the engine for performance, but he managed to work in a flattened third – a blue note. And no matter what he does to the timing, it always has some lope to it, a little syncopation. It's kind of fitting, because Rollie Johnson, the guy I bought it from, was – is – one of the best blues guitarist I know." Joe stood up, wiped his hands and sat by me again. "Much better than J.J. Of course J.J. is a much better mechanic."

"Of course," I said, recalling that J.J. had played briefly with The Average Joes before Joe and I met the first time.

"Remember that story Mary told you about me sitting in with her and the Blues Shepherds out at the state fair? Rollie – 'Rockin' Rollie' Johnson – was the guy I pissed off. Eventually he got over it. We came to an understanding, a mutual, begrudging respect. He eventually left the Shepherds, started his own band." Joe took a deep breath and blew it out. He took my hand, but didn't look at me.

"That last night . . . when we left Pleasant Glen for the audition and things got all haywire . . . it was Rollie's band, Salt Flats Blues, that we ended up replacing. Rollie and his lead singer got into a fight, the rest of the band took sides. They all ended up in jail and we . . . stepped in." Joe and I avoided talking about the night, more than twenty-five years ago, when he left Pleasant Glen for an audition and our romance was torn apart.

"I've always felt like I owed him one. And so did Rollie," Joe said, with a mirthless laugh. "Rollie was – is – immensely talented. Very focused. But he can be an ass. Salt Flats Blues broke up, and Rollie never had his own band again. He always managed to find work, though. I helped him out whenever I could. Nothing ever stuck. He'd quit, or he'd rub people the wrong way and be asked to quit.

"After a while we lost touch, but I'd hear stories. He never changed. Burning bridges faster than he could build them. About fifteen years ago I did a few charity shows that got my name back in the news. Rollie called me looking for a job, said his finances were upside down. I told him those had been one-off gigs for me. I offered to front him some cash until something else came up.

"Rollie got offended. Said he wasn't looking for a hand out, but he had a motorcycle he'd sell me. He spun some story about his old man being a big gearhead. Said he'd been named after Rollie Free and that he'd spent his whole life looking for a Vincent Black Shadow."

Joe looked at me and grinned. "I assume J.J. covered the Black Shadow as well."

I shook my head. "Google."

"Of course. Anyway, Rollie said he'd finally found one. Said it needed a little work. He hated to let it go, but he knew I had a friend who was a mechanic. Said he'd buy it back after things picked up. I ran it by J.J. He thought the price was a little steep – especially buying it sight unseen – but I wanted to help Rollie. And I trusted him."

"But . . . ."

"Yeah, this is a Rapide, not a Black Shadow or even a Black

Lightning. But I didn't know that when I bought it. Rollie probably didn't either. J.J. was here when the boxes arrived."

"Boxes?"

"Rollie *did* say it needed a little work." Joe frowned. "That might have made it more exciting for J.J. Oh, he was pissed at first – or at least he acted like it – cursed Rollie for taking advantage of me, even as he was sorting parts and checking serial numbers.

"This was right after J.J.'s wife died. Trey was, what, two? Restoring this Vincent became an obsession for J.J. I think he used it as an excuse to avoid dealing with his grief. Big George thought so, too, I imagine. But given his history with The Scout, he couldn't say much.

"Then it became kind of a family thing. Miss Irene sent me a picture of the three of them working on this bike. J.J. is kneeling beside it with Trey tucked in front of him. Both of them holding wrenches. Big George is standing behind them, supervising. I think Trey's first word was 'sump,' because they had so much trouble sorting out the oil lines.

"In the meantime, Rollie laid low. I tried to keep tabs on him. I heard rumors about drugs and gambling debts, but nothing from Rollie. Until about five years ago. He was on an early version of Celebrity Rehab. They were finishing up shooting, and Rollie had this long monologue about how he had found religion and was clean and sober. He had big plans to go out on tour . . . and to buy back his motorcycle. The producers contacted me. I agreed to sell the bike back for what I'd paid for it. They convinced me to let Rollie sit in at a show. He'd play a couple numbers with us, then I'd hand over the keys to the bike and he'd ride off into the sunset.

"Rollie showed up for rehearsal, higher than a kite. Couldn't even get his guitar plugged in to the amp. I told him to leave. He got up in my face. 'Fuck you, Captain America. I'll make it back on my own. Some day you'll need someone to catch you and I'm just gonna let you fall on your pompous ass'." Joe frowned, remembering the scene. "Rollie always did have a thing for The Kinks. He told me I'd better take good care of his bike. That he'd be back for it. And then he just . . . disappeared."

"Joe, it's not . . . you did everything you could."

"Maybe. I don't know. The thing is, sometimes I think maybe I did too much. Mary wants to believe he moved to Mexico. Tom thinks he crossed the wrong people."

"What do you think happened to him?"

"Rollie always had to be the center of attention. He didn't care how big the spotlight was, as long as it was shining on him. I'd like to believe he's out there somewhere busking on a street corner, or playing solo in some dive bar for drinks and tips. I'd like to believe he's found something that makes him happy again, like I did." Joe slipped his arm around my waist and kissed me. "Everyone has to find happiness on their own terms, whether it's a motorcycle like The Scout, or a motorcycle-riding woman. Or making music."

"Or a music-making man," I said, returning Joe's kiss.

"I've been thinking a lot about what you said last night," Joe whispered in my ear.

"What I said, or what we did?"

Joe chuckled. "A little of both. Now that I have you back in my life, I want you to know you're a part of *all* of my life." He kissed that spot just below my ear, giving me goosebumps. "I have a proposition for you."

"I like the sound of that," I said, melting into his arms.

"I thought you might." Joe began kissing his way down to my collar bone. "Julie, I want you . . . I need you . . ." I liked where this was going. ". . . to welcome the band when they get here."

"To *what*?" I pulled back so fast I nearly slid off the wall.

"I have a studio session scheduled with that Battle of the Bands group, and there are a couple things I need to finish up before they get here. I was hoping you could help." Joe smirked. "You did say you wanted to be more involved in the business side of my life."

"I did . . . I mean, I do." I figured after all my wheedling I couldn't back out now.

"Great. I'll help Luke set up, listen to a couple things, and then we'll be able to leave for Pleasant Glen around one. All you have to do is point the band toward the studio, okay?"

"Gosh, do you think I'm qualified for this level of work?"

"Hey, you gotta start somewhere. Of course, if you think it's too tough . . . ."

"I think I'll manage. What's the pay for this? Union scale?"

"We'll discuss remuneration once the job's done." Joe gave me a kiss that was far above my pay grade, but I didn't complain.

Chapter 23

After another half a cup of coffee and some intensely enjoyable wage negotiations, Joe was on his way to the studio and I was in the kitchen wondering what I had gotten myself into.

Joe had built his studio at the height of his popularity. He had been looking to spend more time at home and to exert more control over his music while the record label was pushing him to chase trends. He also saw it as an investment, a business he could fall back on after his career faded. While he wasn't topping the charts anymore, Joe's career was still going strong. Instead of being a money-maker, the studio had become one more way for him to nurture local talent. Joe occasionally sat in on recordings or offered advice, but for the most part he left his sound engineer, Luke, in charge of the business side.

"There's a young group coming in this morning – Thunder Pigs. They came in second at a college battle of the bands Luke judged. He said they had more talent than the winners, but fewer beer-drinking fans. You know how that goes," Joe said. I thought back to my days as a waitress at The Bar, when The Average Joes had been blessed with both talent and fans. Bob always said the only thing better than a good bar band was a bar band with fans who liked to drink . . . and spend money.

I was sitting at the kitchen island going over details for Steve and Michael's party when I heard a car pull up. A tall, skinny boy with long, wavy hair that brushed his shoulders came up onto the porch to meet me, while three more boys and a girl wrestled instruments out of the trunk.

"Hi! Are you guys Thunder Pigs?" I asked. The boy nodded. His hair hid half his face, but I saw one corner of his mouth turn up in a quick smile. He shrugged, then stuffed his hands in his pockets and swayed slightly.

"Max," he said, glancing up through a curtain of hair. His voice was so quiet it took me a moment to process what I heard.

"Oh! I'm Julie!" I stuck my hand out to shake his, just as he pulled a pair of drumsticks from his back pocket. He blushed, shifted the drumsticks to his other hand, and quickly shook mine.

"Drummer," he mumbled. I think.

"That's cool," I said. The corner of his mouth lifted again, and he shrugged. This job was tougher than I expected. I pointed to his t-shirt. "Wow! I love the Offspring." He looked down at his shirt, then up at me and arched an eyebrow. "Well, you know, their early stuff, anyway." He blinked slowly. "I have a daughter who is about your age. She's the one who . . . ."

Max nodded and sighed. I felt like we were really connecting. Bullet, apparently more accustomed to welcoming Joe's clients than I was, bumped his head against Max's knee. Max reached down to pet him, then looked at me for permission.

"He would love it if you would pet him." As soon as Max started scratching Bullet's ears, the barn cats swarmed him as well. Out by the car, the others began arguing loudly. Max looked up at me and sighed.

"Studio?" he ask/mumbled.

"In the barn. The door is around the other side. Bullet will show you the way."

Bullet barked once, then led Max down the stairs. Max nodded as they approached the other boys and Bullet circled them, rounding up his flock. A boy with buzz-cut dark hair, ruddy cheeks and a purple bow tie started laughing.

"Leave it to Max to keep us on time," he said, looking back at me. "Get it? He's the drummer, and he's keeping us on time. Because that's what drummers do – keep time. Ha! I got a million of 'em!" Bullet barked and pushed at the boy's ankles with his long nose, keeping the herd moving.

As they disappeared around the side of the barn, quiet settled back across the yard, like the calm after a storm. One of the cats sat next to me and stared toward the barn, as if he too was flustered. Thunder Pig's arrival reminded me more of greeting Emily's high school friends than Gary's colleagues. I wasn't sure if it was their age or vocation – Mary and the Blues Shepherds had a similar exuberance – that made the businessmen seem stuffy.

Back inside, I checked my email and found two new inquiries for event planning. As much as I wanted to be more a part of Joe's life, I knew I couldn't let it consume me. I had let that happen with Gary and I didn't want to repeat that mistake. I needed to maintain my own identity and interests. I sent off a couple quick responses for my "me" job, before returning to my "Joe" job. If Gary hosted clients – or Emily had friends over – my next move would be to provide snacks.

A quick inventory of Joe's pantry turned up the usual staples: cream of mushroom soup, a box of macaroni and cheese, Sterzings potato chips, and a jar of Boetje's mustard. A more aggressive search turned up peanut butter, crisped rice cereal and both chocolate and butterscotch chips. I figured Thunder Pigs would appreciate Scotcheroos much more than the artisan crackers and tins of pâté and caviar Sophia had stocked for company.

My phone rang while I was licking the spatula. Helen's name flashed on the screen. I weighed my options. On the one hand, I knew Helen wouldn't call me during her sacrosanct business call time unless it was important. On the other hand, the melted chocolate/butterscotch frosting was still warm and yummy and very, very messy. I sighed and tapped the speakerphone feature, leaving a small smudge on the screen.

"Julie! Thank goodness. I thought I'd have to leave a message and . . . that just wouldn't do."

I had rarely heard Helen this rattled. "Is everything okay, Helen?"

"Not entirely, dear. I had to excuse myself from a rather uninspired discussion with some art guild members. Honestly! There's so much more to Frida Kahlo than those unfortunate eyebrows."

"Helen?" Somehow I didn't think she had called me just to vent about misguided art critics. Something – other than Frida Kahlo's unibrow – had Helen flustered. Flustered bad.

"I'm sorry my dear. First it was Georgia O'Keeffe and her 'pornographic flowers,' then it was poor Frida, and on top of it all, I received a text from Gary saying he wouldn't be able to return with me to Pleasant Glen this evening. A *text*! He knew I was in a meeting and he chose to *text* me rather than call me in person. He's becoming more like his father every day." Helen huffed angrily. "Julie dear, I know it's a terrible imposition, but could I possibly ride with you and . . . your friend?"

My initial, good girl reaction was to say yes – especially since I liked Helen and because she sounded distraught. It was only after that word left my mouth that I realized I had just agreed to a two-hour car ride with my soon-to-be ex-mother-in-law and my most-likely-future-husband. I assured Helen I was glad to help out and that we would pick her up at one-thirty.

The potential for awkwardness hung over me as I cut – and sampled – the still gooey bars. Fortified by the sugar rush and hoping the treats would act as a bribe, I went out to the studio to break the news to Joe.

Thunder Pigs were doing a cover of Led Zeppelin's "Rock and Roll" when I snuck into the control room. Behind the drum kit, Max was a blur of long hair and flying drumsticks.

"He seemed so quiet when he got here," I said, surprised by the transformation.

Joe grinned. "I thought he was mute! Wondered what Luke had got me into. But he's good. They're all good. Kinda makes me . . . ." His turned his attention back to the window and watched the band.

"You want to stay, don't you?" I asked.

"You already had to put up with me playing with the Shepherds." Joe bit his lip. "Besides, I'm just here to observe and give moral support."

Luke snorted. "It's your studio, dude. I just run the controls. Besides, these kids would freak if they had the chance to play with a living legend." Joe appeared to be thinking it over. "That is, if you think you can keep up with them, old man."

Joe laughed, but took the bait. "Maybe for a song or two. What do you think, Julie? Could we stay another hour or so? Really, how much trouble could Miss Irene get into . . . never mind. We should go. We should already be there."

I sensed a way out of my awkward predicament. "This isn't about Miss Irene, or me. Or even you, Joe Davenport. These kids remind me of Emily's friends. You should stay and work with them. We can drive separately. It will be nice to have two cars in Pleasant Glen for running errands."

Joe hugged me and gave me a kiss that left me wishing I didn't have to leave.

"Wait a minute," Joe said, loosening his embrace. "You brought me treats *and* you're letting me stay behind? You're a sweet girl, but this is a little bit too sweet – even for you. Are you breaking up with me?"

Luke signaled the band to meet him in the hallway, then picked up the Scotcheroos. "You two need to get a private room if this leads to makeup sex." He stopped in the doorway. "And if you're not . . . Julie, my number is on my card. Gimme a call some time."

"The control room *is* soundproof," Joe said, after Luke closed the door.

"I'll keep that in mind." I kissed a smudge of chocolate off Joe's lips before my guilty conscience got the better of me. "I do have an ulterior motive. Helen, Gary's mom, needs a ride to Pleasant Glen and I'm not sure I can handle being in the Mini Cooper with both of you for that long. Or – even worse – the cab of your truck."

Joe chuckled. "That could be a little awkward. Of course, we could take the Jag." Sophia had goaded him into buying the sporty, red coupe, saying he needed to play up his rock star status.

"I'm not going to make Helen ride in the trunk. And I'm not

riding there either."

"Just trying to be a problem solver." Joe grinned. "I promise I will be on my best behavior."

"I know you will, and I'm sure she will be too. It's just . . . she sounded upset on the phone. I think it would be best if we had a little alone time." Best for Helen, maybe, but I wasn't exactly looking forward to it. "So you stay, have fun, mold young minds. Just be home before the street lights come on."

"I was a farm kid, remember? What happens after the street lights come on?"

"You'll just have to wait and see. But I promise it will be worth it."

Chapter 24

As soon as I reached the end of Joe's driveway, I realized I had made a terrible mistake. Without Joe there to distract me, my mind was free to wander, pausing only when it stumbled across some half-buried fear. *I was going to be alone in a car for more than two hours with my soon-to-be ex-mother-in-law.* By the time I reached Prairie's Edge Estates, I considered turning around. *Two hours of listening to Helen recite Gary's good points.* Then I remembered how happy Joe looked in the recording studio. I could handle this by myself. I was just making up things to worry about. *I had no reason to feel guilty for leaving Gary.*

I *didn't* feel guilty for leaving Gary. I felt guilty for disappointing Helen.

As if to underscore this realization, a semi passed me, leaving my Mini Cooper shuddering in its wake. Helen had been my *friend* before she was my mother-in-law, but she was Gary's *mom.* How could she not be disappointed in me?

Helen would never come right out and tell me she was disappointed, of course. She was much too kind to say such a thing. That was one of the things I admired about her. Helen was thoughtful, sophisticated and confident – all the things I aspired to be. The only thing I didn't admire about Helen was the way she put up with Richard's womanizing. That was one thing I wouldn't emulate, even if it did disappoint Helen.

Now that I understood – or *thought* I understood – the

source of my anxiety, I could concentrate less on my overactive imagination – *what if Dear Abby took Helen's side in an advice column-gone-viral?* – and concentrate more on finding Gary's condo.

Gary had moved to a newly constructed, planned community featuring neighborhoods defined by architecture. I drove through a cluster of prairie-style homes, took a left after the craftsman cottages, and pulled onto a street lined with San Francisco-style row houses. The gingerbread details were adorable, but the lack of visible street numbers was not. I turned around when I reached the brick Tudors. This time through, Helen was standing outside waiting for me.

"Julie, dear, I was beginning to worry! It's all so . . . ." Helen looked around at the uniform buildings, as if she were searching for the most fitting adjective. While there were quite a few I wanted to supply, I decided to play nice.

"Clever? Trendy?" I suggested.

Helen tilted her head and frowned. "I was going to say pretentious . . . but to each his own, dear." She took another look around. "Oh, there's a certain charm, I suppose, but there's no personality. No individuality." She snorted. "No house numbers for heaven's sake. It's against the homeowners association bylaws. Don't even get me started on the mandates for holiday decorations and garbage cans."

Helen picked up her bags and headed towards the car. "Shall we go, dear?"

I had expected her to tell me how cozy the condo would be for a couple of empty nesters. I had expected a guilt-filled tour of the condo. Now that it seemed Helen was *not* planning on giving me a guilt-filled tour of Gary's condo, I perversely wanted one. I dropped a couple of hints while I loaded her luggage, then flat-out asked to see the condo I had heard so much about.

"Oh . . . of course." Helen checked her watch. "Perhaps a quick look . . . ." Helen stepped away from the car, smoothed her already perfect hair, and squared her shoulders. The transformation couldn't have been any more striking if she had spun in a circle, called "Oh, mighty Isis," and stripped down to a swim suit and golden lasso, à la Linda Carter-era Wonder Woman. In a blink of an eye Helen, my mother-in-law, became Mrs. Helen Westbrook, professional real estate agent. I had witnessed this change many times when I helped with open houses before she and Richard moved to Florida.

Open houses in Pleasant Glen are social events, attended more often by curious neighbors and bored retirees than people actually looking to buy. Where Richard saw snoops and freeloaders attracted by refreshments, Helen saw potential sellers who would one day need to downsize. Helen made every visitor feel at home – helping them see how this house, *this very house*, could be their perfect home. Meanwhile, Richard stayed at the office to handle the paperwork and – apparently – his secretary.

Helen was in full, professional realtor mode during our walk-through – gracious and charming, yet impersonal enough to avoid being chummy. Her recitation of the condo's selling points was almost as bland as the condo itself. The polite banter and small talk continued as we made our way through the greater Des Moines area. It wasn't until we were east of Altoona, out where the traffic thinned and housing developments gave way to farm fields, that the conversation turned more personal.

"Do you plan on moving in with the musician, dear?"

Helen dropped that little bomb into the conversation without changing her tone of voice or turning away from the window. I wondered if she realized she had said anything aloud. I took my time, considering my answer carefully. I didn't want to give Helen false hope about me reconciling with Gary, but I couldn't outright lie to her either.

"Eventually. Right now he's still traveling a lot and I have some big projects I'm working on."

"I do hope you'll forgive my impertinence. I know it's really none of my business." Helen turned toward me and smiled, placing her hand on the console between us. "I've always liked you, Julie. I worry about you. Whether or not you are my daughter-in-law, that won't change." This was the first time I had heard Helen come remotely close to admitting that Gary and I were splitting. "I don't want to see you rush into anything." Or not.

"Joe and I have been in love for more than twenty-five years. I hardly think we're 'rushing into' anything."

Helen raised an eyebrow. "You were *separated* for more than twenty-five years, as I understand it. You've currently been seeing each other for what, three months?"

"Four." Ish. If we were being generous. While I didn't want to lie to Helen, I wasn't above stretching the truth a little.

"Oh, I have no doubt that you are in love. I recognize the signs. But Julie, dear, love alone is no guarantee of happiness or security. Your relationship with Gary may not be perfect, but he does care for you. Love can not provide safety, financial security, or social standing. I should know." She returned her attention to the landscape outside her window. When she spoke again, her voice was quiet and wistful. "I married for love once."

"Surely you and Richard can . . . ."

Helen gave me a puzzled look. "Richard? Oh, no, dear. I didn't mean Richard. I was married once before him, to the love of my life." Her voice turned bitter. "For all the good that did us."

"I'm so sorry. Gary never . . . ."

"Gary doesn't know. No one did, my dear. Miss Irene may have suspected, but she would never pry."

Several miles passed before Helen continued her story.

"James was my high school sweetheart. We planned to marry right after graduation. Of course, my family did not approve – of James, or of our plans. They threatened to disown me, and they did. What did we care? We were young and in love. We moved to Kansas City – I had a scholarship to the Art Institute. James got a factory job with plenty of overtime. We found an apartment on the edge of campus that wasn't completely run down. We were happy. We were in love. And soon we were expecting a child.

"Angela was born before final exams that Spring. It was an easy pregnancy, an easy birth. She was such a happy baby. We were such a happy family. I didn't know my heart could hold so much love.

"My professors were wonderfully understanding. They made accommodations for me to complete my classes. I often took Angela to the studio with me while James picked up an extra shift at work. She charmed everyone.

"One night, James stayed home with the baby while I went in to finish up the last of my finals. They were cuddled together asleep on the bed when I left." Helen gave me a sad smile. "As soon as I heard the sirens, I knew. It was an old building. The fire escapes shook in the wind. They could never have . . . . I'm sure the smoke . . . ." Helen dabbed at her nose with a tissue. I struggled to see the road through my tears.

"James' parents blamed me. I blamed myself. My family figured I got what I deserved. I had no desire to stay in Kansas City and I couldn't go home to Dubuque. My grandmother, fearing an even bigger scandal than the elopement, arranged for me to live with her sister in Pleasant Glen. But there were conditions. Grandmother's generosity always came at a price. I took back my maiden name and James and Angela were never mentioned again. It was like they never existed.

"I transferred to Pleasant Glen College and joined a sorority. That's where I met Beatrice. It's also how I met Richard's mother. She was one of our alumni advisers. My . . . experience had changed me. I was more mature, more serious than the other girls. I was just the type of wife she wanted for her son. I knew I could never find another James, but Richard could provide safety and respectability.

"And so, just a year after I buried the two loves of my life, I married again. Soon I was pregnant. I vowed to do whatever it took to protect my child and make him successful."

I shuddered. Parts of Helen's story sounded all too familiar.

"So when we met, you picked me out for Gary, just like Richard's mom picked you for him," I said. It was more of an accusation than a question.

"What? Oh my, no!" Helen looked so shocked by my suggestion I wasn't sure if I should be relieved or insulted. It was one thing to be in an arranged marriage. It was quite another thing to be considered not good enough for the arrangement.

Helen sat quietly, picking at imaginary lint on her slacks. "Well, not at first," she admitted. That soothed my ego somewhat. "Of course you were just the type of woman I wanted for Gary – smart, considerate, charming – not at all like the type of girls he chose to date. Not at all like his fiance, Pamela. I never cared for her. She was much too ambitious. But she was Gary's choice, and I respected his decision." She shook her head and muttered, "Even if I knew he would regret it someday.

"Actually, dear, I was a little concerned when Gary started pursuing you so soon after their breakup. I knew he had a reputation. I had listened to many teary ex-girlfriends, endured the frosty glares from their mothers. I didn't want that to happen to you. And I said so to Gary.

"When he continued to court you with such sincerity, I believed he saw in you the same qualities I did. You changed him, Julie. You were good for him. And together you built a good life. A safe, secure life. You two seemed happy, or at least content. If there was a spark missing, I didn't notice. Perhaps I had forgotten what true love looked like. Perhaps Gary never knew.

"He honestly thought he was doing you a favor when he . . . interfered in your relationship with Joe. It was self-serving, yes, but his intentions were good.

"He was wrong, Julie. I was wrong. You're not like me. You have always been much more like Miss Irene. You need that spark. I didn't realize how unhappy you were. I'm terribly sorry."

"What made you change your mind?" I asked.

"I didn't know what he had done, Julie. I didn't realize how much Gary was like his father.

"When Richard and I moved to Florida, when he saw I was serious about leaving him, he made a commitment to rebuilding our marriage. He has since reverted to his old ways. Again. When I returned to Pleasant Glen, I thought that if I couldn't save my marriage, maybe I could save yours. But this development between Miss Irene and Big George has made me take a closer look at all our relationships. They are unconventional, to be sure, but I've never doubted their love for each other."

"Even now? It seems to me like Miss Irene is doing everything she can to push Big George away."

"Irene is scared, Julie. I'm sure you can see that."

"Yes, but . . . ."

"No, his health issue wasn't caused by their . . . activities, but it did remind her of his mortality. She's trying to keep him safe. She's willing to sacrifice her happiness for his safety. She's miserable, Julie, and so is George."

"Could you talk to her?

Helen shook her head. "I've tried, dear. But you know how stubborn Irene can be. She has to learn for herself. We all do, unfortunately. It's going to take more than words to convince her." Helen toyed absentmindedly with her pearl necklace as we approached the outskirts of Pleasant Glen. A smile slowly spread across Helen's face. "Don't give up hope, dear."

I felt bad leaving Helen alone at our – Gary's – old house, but she assured me she was meeting a friend for dinner and had plenty of work to keep her busy. Besides, she said, Emily would be home soon to keep her company. And I was expecting company of my own.

Joe was not waiting for me when I got back to my apartment – not that I expected him to be – but Beatrice and her sisters were sitting under the tree in the back yard. Francine and Jean looked like younger, hipper versions of Beatrice – who looked like an older, more frowzy version of Miss Irene. The twins wore coordinating green and orange Phiting Pheasant sweatshirts with contrasting orange and green flasks. Soon after we were introduced, a mid-1960s Mustang roared up the alley, the horn tooting "La Cucaracha" as it pulled in behind the garage.

"That's our ride!" the twins said in unison. They looked at each other and nodded, sharing some silent, twin communication.

"Don't do anything we wouldn't do!" Francine said.

"Not that our little Bea-scout ever would," Jean added. Their laughter trailed them until it was mercifully cut off by the sound of car doors slamming and tires squealing.

Beatrice ignored her sister's behavior and eagerly filled me in on what I'd missed while in Des Moines. Things had gone from bad to worse, she said. Miss Irene had continued her early bird bingo habit and Big George – whose hours and duties at the shop had been cut back – had started going to the bakery for breakfast.

"Fun fact: They serve coffee – *caffeinated* coffee – at bingo," Beatrice said. "My source tells me attendance increased drastically this week, as did the quality of the coffee. On the flip side, the breakfast crowd down at the bakery has taken a hit. Seems Velma has been too busy flirting with a certain mechanic to pay much attention to what goes on behind the counter. Between the burnt toast and, quote, 'an invasion of gossipy old hens,' some of the male regulars have become avid bingo players.

"In other words, things are going according to plan!" Beatrice said with a giggle. I thought her giggle sounded more than a bit ominous, and I still had no idea what "plan" she had in mind.

Joe finally arrived around 9 o'clock – long after the street lights had come on, but before I called out the National Guard to search for him. He said he had enjoyed playing with Thunder Pigs, but realized he would rather be spending time with me. He even brought me Krispie Kreme donuts as an apology.

What can I say? The man knows the way to my heart.

Chapter 25

Miss Irene's "Posh and Pamper" day was the result of high-stakes arbitration that made me consider giving up event planning to do something less dangerous – like bomb disposal. It was a compromise, and like all compromises, it left both sides feeling they had been screwed.

Miss Irene's daughters were thrilled when she called to tell them about the wedding. They were quick to congratulate the happy couple, and even quicker to assure their mother they would be honored to be her bridesmaids.

Miss Irene said that after a nearly 50-year engagement, the wedding was merely a formality. She laughed and told them she thought she was a little too old for bridesmaids and that they were, quite frankly, a little too old to *be* bridesmaids.

All three girls hung up crying.

Beatrice called back early the next morning to apologize for her sisters' behavior, and to reassure her mother that all three girls were overjoyed that she and Big George would no longer be "living in sin." Besides, Bea said, the title "Matron of Honor" sounded much more sophisticated and suited her "to a T." She hung up before her mother could protest.

The twins called back before noon to apologize for their sister's behavior, and to tell Miss Irene how happy they were Big George was "finally making an honest woman of her." Besides, they said, the term "attendants" was much less age-ist and suited them "to a T." They hung up before their mother could protest.

Miss Irene called all three girls at dinner-time to thank them for their concern and to tell them she and Big George would be the only two members of the wedding party.

Two days later, Beatrice emailed her mother a list of online retailers specializing in wedding gowns for the mature bride. She also included a link to a mint green gown with a ruffled, organza skirt and high-necked lace jacket that was more suited for the mother of the bride than the daughter of the bride. But then again, so was Bea.

Three days later, the twins emailed their mother a list of hip, designer wedding gowns and a link to a body-hugging, red sequined dress that was more suited to cabaret singers than bridal attendants – regardless of their age.

Miss Irene emailed her daughters a link to wedding chapels in Kahoka, Missouri, and told them she and Big George might elope.

Miss Irene's daughters emailed back saying: A. It wasn't 1940; B. She and Big George were well over the legal age of consent to marry in Iowa; C. If Miss Irene and Big George *did* elope the girls wouldn't attend; and D. If they *did* elope they should at least have the decency to go to Las Vegas because the twins already had the red sequined dresses.

J.J. pointed out that there was no such drama coming from the men in the family. Miss Irene pointed out that if he didn't keep his observations to himself, he would – as the youngest of their combined children – be appointed ring-bearer and would be required to wear a suit with short pants.

I reminded Miss Irene that every little girl dreams of a fairy tale wedding filled with acres of silk and tulle, bushels of roses, a horse-drawn carriage and at least two swans. Miss Irene reminded me that the little girls in question had already enjoyed fairy tale weddings of their own – financed by her – and had orchestrated fairy tale weddings for their own little girls.

I convinced Miss Irene the girls just wanted to show their support for her and to enjoy a little female bonding. I suggested a spa day filled with activities designed to pamper and indulge their feminine fantasies. Miss Irene put me in charge of planning the spa day and thanked me for volunteering to chaperone the group.

Neither of us doubted that Beatrice and the twins would show up at the wedding in their gowns.

The girls insisted on keeping the spa day even after Miss Irene called off the wedding, saying it would help keep her spirits up. I suspected it was more about keeping *their* spirits up, but to be honest, I was looking forward to a manicure myself. Besides, we all hoped Miss Irene would come to her senses and the wedding weekend would proceed as planned.

Miss Irene's day of pampering was scheduled to begin with a champagne breakfast at Glen View Grille – part of a package deal that included the rehearsal dinner and catering for the reception. The Grille held fast to their non-refundable deposit policy until Thursday afternoon, when a befuddled bridge player – upon leaving the weekly game in the lounge – turned the main dining room into a drive-thru. The brunch was canceled and the rehearsal-turned-family dinner switched to catered. But the the deposit was not refunded.

Given Miss Irene's recent embargo on caffeine – at least in her house – her daughters opted to have their pre-spa breakfast at the bakery, where the coffee flowed almost as freely as the gossip. Miss Irene said she'd have breakfast at the Legion. Joe and I planned to enjoy breakfast in bed.

Planned was the operative word there. We were barely awake and hadn't had time to enjoy much of anything when Miss Irene called. She said there had been an "incident" at the Legion Hall and she needed me to escort her to the spa. Given that the Legion was a block from the spa and that we would be walking right past the bakery – and her daughters – I was suspicious. And worried.

"Incident," I had learned, was Miss Irene's understated way of describing most near-disasters. Her recent run-in with the high school principal, for example, had been downgraded to "incident" when she told her kids about it. The time Big George's wife had accidentally caused the manual transmission shop truck to roll over Frank was described to me as an "incident."

The closest I came to breakfast was Joe singing "Black Coffee In Bed." God, I love 80s music. I jumped through the shower, gratefully accepted the travel mug filled with coffee he handed me, took a drink while he waited, then kissed him goodbye. God, I love that man.

I found a parking space catty cornered from the Legion, overlooking the town square. A crowd was gathered around the quaint fountain in the center of the square. Most of them had their backs to me, but I recognized Pleasant Glen's mayor by the way his deep comb-over waved at me in the breeze.

Tony Borglund had become a successful mayor by surrounding himself with people smarter than him and not interfering with their work. Still, he occasionally liked to publicly flex his mayoral-ness, and today seemed to be one of those days.

While Tony pointed and shouted – thunderous rumbles that carried through my closed windows – members of the crowd nodded and milled about. Apparently unappeased by this response, Tony threw his arms in the air, wheeled around, and stomped in my direction. The crowd followed, merging to fit the narrow sidewalk and clearing my line of sight to the fountain. Mounds of soap bubbles filled the lower basin of the fountain – the traditional prank marking the first win of the Phiting Pheasant football season. Every year, Pleasant Glen officials pretend to be outraged when this occurs. And every year a group of PGHS students are rounded up at random – regardless of guilt – and sentenced to community service.

As the mayor and his cohort neared, I eased my car door open and strained to make out what Tony was saying. I fully expected to hear something along the lines of "tar and feathers" or "grab the pitchforks and light the torches." Faced with the oncoming angry mob, my guilty conscience went into overdrive. I racked my brain to think of anyone who could account for my whereabouts between the time I spoke with Beatrice and the time Joe arrived. I cursed myself for buying the economy-size bottle of Mr. Bubble when Emily was 7 years old. I wondered if shuffling political yard signs after an election was illegal or just immoral. Although if pressed, I would deny any knowledge of such an event occurring in the fall of 1983.

I had decided to blame the whole thing – whatever it may be – on Vanessa, when Tony veered off the sidewalk and headed toward the Statue of Liberty replica. The crowd re-assembled at the star-shaped, hip-high, limestone planter which held a six-foot tall, concrete plinth which supported the eight-and-a-half-foot tall, bronze statue. Lady Liberty had stood on this corner facing the Legion Hall since the Boy Scouts donated her to the city in 1950. Today, in addition to her crown and torch, she sported a jaunty tam-o'-shanter and matching kilt in the distinctive orange and green plaid of the Galloping Glennies.

While Tony and company peered up Lady Liberty's skirt, I slipped out of my car and made my escape. I cut across the intersection, weaving around cars that were crawling past the square while their drivers gawked at the spectacle.

No wonder Miss Irene wanted an escort, I thought. *This prank had her name written all over it.* I hopped the curb and nearly collided with a diminutive, disheveled patron stumbling out the door of the Legion.

"Julie, dear? Is that you?" Miss Irene asked in a weak voice. She looked to my left, then my right, and then up and down. "Be a dear and try to come into focus, would you?" Her eyes were magnified behind bottle-thick lenses set in chunky, black plastic frames. She had a bump the size of a goose egg in the center of her forehead, and her hair stood on end. Her white cardigan had bingo dauber ink smudges, the knees of her polyester pants were dirty, and one shoe was untied.

Correction: This prank would *have had her fingerprints all over it if she hadn't been abducted by the aliens from the movie "Cocoon" and replaced by a pod person.*

"Miss Irene! What happened?" I steadied her, then bent down to tie her shoe and brush coffee grounds from her slacks.

"Ohhhhh, that blasted Kenny Rees was tinkering with the bingo ball blower machine. I took a B-15 to the head! Broke my glasses. Someone left these trifocals in the lost and found." Miss Irene tilted her chin this way and that. "I see why, now. Damn things don't work. Kenny took my glasses, said he'd fix 'em."

Miss Irene groaned, closed her eyes, and took hold of my elbow. "You're going to have to be my seeing-eye dog 'till he gets back."

"Are you sure you want Mr. Rees messing around with your glasses?" I asked, as we slowly made our way across the street. "I mean, what with the ball blower and all. I'm sure Big George would . . . ."

"Don't you think I thought of that?" Miss Irene snapped at me, nearly losing her balance in the process. "I called George as soon as I regained consciousness, but he didn't answer. Probably down at the shop, tinkering with that damn motorcycle. And after he promised me he'd take it easy, too."

Miss Irene continued to mutter, but a commotion in front of the bakery distracted me. Deputy Doug was writing in his citation book, while Francine rummaged through a purse the size of a carry-on bag. Jean and Beatrice hovered nearby.

"But Officer, I have a handicap parking permit in here somewhere, I swear," Francine said as she pulled things from her bag and set them carefully on the hood of her canary-yellow, Thunderbird convertible.

"Honest, Officer," Jean said. "Her doctor nipped when he should have tucked, and now one butt cheek is slightly higher than the other. Very painful."

"See? Although I don't think it's as noticeable when I'm wearing slacks." Francine turned to give Deputy Doug a better view of her . . . injury. The young deputy shuddered, then went back to writing out the parking ticket. "Tell him, Mother," Francine said, catching sight of us.

Deputy Doug looked up and frowned. "She's your mother?" he asked, pointing at Miss Irene. The girls nodded in unison. Deputy Doug ripped the ticket out of his notebook and tore it up.

"Officer, arrest that woman!" Mayor Borglund yelled from the middle of Main Street. This was shaping up to be the most exciting day downtown Pleasant Glen had seen in quite some time.

"Found it!" Francine shouted, pulling a blue and white parking placard from the depths of her purse.

"But she's got a . . . ." Deputy Doug stammered.

"Not that one, *that* one," the mayor said, pointing at Miss Irene. "Wanton desecration of a national monument. Defiling of public property. Mocking the very foundations upon which this great nation of ours was . . . founded." Borglund was red in the face and waggling his finger at Miss Irene as he continued his tirade. "Sacrilege! Hi-jinks! *Vannnnn-dalism!*"

"Mayor Borglund, you can't seriously believe a 90-year-old woman had anything to do with . . . that," I said, pointing towards the Statue of Liberty. An extension ladder leaned against the plinth, abandoned, while city crew members in hard hats directed the approach of a bucket truck.

"Marauder! Hooligan! Philistine!"

"Sir, with all due respect, our mother couldn't have had anything to do with that," Beatrice said calmly. "She retired to bed shortly after 8 p.m., and was sleeping soundly when I checked on her at 10."

Mayor Borglund crossed his arms and snorted. He looked Miss Irene over from top to bottom, leaning in for a closer look at her glasses. Miss Irene tilted her chin searching for the portion of lens that would allow her to see him clearly at that distance.

"Hmph. I heard you'd gone round the bend, but I didn't believe . . . ." Borglund turned towards Francine and Jean. "What about the 'Troublemint Twins,' here? Don't think I've forgotten that time you stuffed me into a locker back in junior high."

"We took in the ball game," said Francine.

"Never miss a chance to shake our pompoms," added Jean, with a shimmy.

"Then stopped by the Glen View Lounge . . . ."

"Some of the old gang can't hold their liquor any better than they did in high school!"

"And then went back to the hotel . . . ."

"Where we made margaritas and sat pool side until . . . ." Jean looked at her twin and giggled.

"Until . . . ." Francine looked at Jean and giggled.

"Until . . . ." Mayor Borglund prodded.

"Until we got kicked out!" Both girls hooted with laughter.

"It must have been around midnight," Francine said. "Just ask the night manager."

"I'm sure he'll remember us," Jean said. "We were skinny dipping."

Mayor Borglund went pale. Deputy Doug looked like he might pass out.

"If you have no further baseless accusations, gentlemen, we are late for an appointment," Miss Irene said, tugging my arm.

"Just a cotton-picking minute!" Borglund didn't give up that easily. "What about you, Beatrice? If your mother was asleep, who can verify your whereabouts?"

"Oh puh-leeze, Borgy!" Jean said. "You can't seriously think Beatrice would have anything to do with . . ."

"With *anything*," Francine said, waving dismissively.

"Not Boring Bea . . . ." Francine said.

"Not Vanilla Bea . . . ."

"Bookworm Bea . . . ."

The twins looked at each other and frowned, then turned to scowl at the Mayor.

"Be-AT-riss?" asked Jean.

"Be SER-ious!" said Francine.

With cheerleader-like precision they turned and marched towards the salon.

"Come along, ladies . . . ." Francine called over her shoulder to us.

"We mustn't be late!" said Jean.

Chapter 26

Mayor Borglund, unaccustomed to being snubbed, sputtered and scowled at the twins' backsides as they sashayed down the block. Deputy Doug quickly averted his eyes from their swaying hips.

"Well Mayor, unless there are any other members of my family you would like to falsely accuse . . . ." Beatrice said with uncharacteristic sharpness. "I believe my mother needs to get off her feet."

Miss Irene's trifocal-induced vertigo had returned, and she swayed slightly. Beatrice and I propped her up between us and followed in the twins' wake. The two sisters carried on an animated discussion. Occasionally they would glance back and I could catch a word or two out of context.

"Blessed are the meek . . ." Jean said.

Francine nodded. "Bea-atitudes."

". . . Bea-witched?"

"Bea-wildered . . . ."

". . . Bea-mused?"

"Bea-guiled!"

I seemed to be the only one bothered by the twin's behavior. Once or twice, I saw Bea's lips twitch in a barely suppressed grin. Miss Irene continued to sway and moan. She stumbled over an arrow painted on the sidewalk to welcome clients to the salon and the twins rushed to help us catch her.

"Miss Irene, why don't you take off those glasses," I asked, frustrated by too little caffeine and too much drama.

"Don't be foolish!" Miss Irene snapped. "You know I can't see a thing without glasses!"

I wanted to point out that right now she couldn't see a thing *with* glasses, either, but I knew better than to try her patience. The twins, however, seemed to be more willing to press their mother's buttons.

"Someone woke up on the wrong side of the bed," Francine said.

"Someone woke up in an *empty* bed," Jean corrected.

"Someone woke up with an empty *head* and should keep their opinions to themselves," Miss Irene said.

"All I'm saying is you haven't been yourself since you froze out Big George," Francine said. "I never thought I'd say this to my mother, but you need to get . . . ."

"Ladies! I was beginning to wor . . . . Oh, my goodness, Irene! What happened to your hea . . . . Get her inside this instant, girls!" I don't know how much of the conversation Stacy had heard, but I was glad she interrupted when she did. Once inside the salon, Stacy, the salon owner and a former EMT – and, some said, former Special Ops or Mossad – examined the bump on Miss Irene's head. She ruled out a concussion but suggested Miss Irene stay downstairs where she could keep an eye on her. Francine and Jean linked arms with Beatrice and whisked her upstairs to the spa, leaving me with their mother. Miss Irene and I were scheduled for hair and nails and escorted to a quiet alcove separated from the rest of the salon by frosted glass dividers.

Miss Irene's attitude improved once the loaner glasses were removed, her hair washed and feet massaged. The extra-large mimosa she chugged may have also helped. Soon after they lowered the hair dryer hood over her curlers, Miss Irene was "resting her eyes" and snoring softly. While I waited for my "flame-ingo" pink painted nails to dry, I watched the other clients who had clustered at the front window for Lady Liberty's strip tease. I was about to join them when a chicly dressed woman stepped into our room.

"Helen! I almost mistook you for a young Audrey Hepburn!" Miss Irene said, making me wonder just how little she could see without glasses.

"Thank you, Irene. I felt like trying something different today. New leaf, new look . . . new life!" Helen performed a graceful pirouette and posed, laughing the whole time. She maintained her classic black and white color scheme, but today she was wearing a pair of fitted cigarette pants that emphasized her slender waist and a black-and-white striped, boat neck blouse. Instead of her usual three-inch heels, she was wearing a pair of black Keds tennis shoes that I was certain were Emily's. Her signature gray pearls were noticeably absent. Her silver hair hung loosely, held back from her face by a red silk scarf used as a headband. Noticing my gaze, she touched the scarf and apologized.

"I hope you don't mind, dear. I wanted to celebrate with a little pop of color."

"Not at all! You wear it beautifully. You know, that scarf came from the art gallery . . . ." In fact, it was the scarf Gary had over-bid on at a gallery fundraiser as a guilt gift the first time I suspected him of cheating on me. It was the scarf I had worn as a sign of defiance the first time I exerted my independence. I had left it with a pile of odds and ends I stored in Emily's room.

Helen's eyes sparkled. "That is part of the reason I borrowed it," she said. "Oh, my! I have so much news to share! But first . . . ." Helen reached into her black leather Burberry tote and pulled out a bottle of champagne. While my tastes run more toward Three Buck Chuck, I recognized the label and knew it was a much better vintage than you could purchase in Pleasant Glen – even from the locked display at Hy-Vee.

"Irene, I wanted you to be the first to know. I've . . . Julie, darling, would you be a dear and go check on Beatrice and the girls? I overheard them mention something about getting a Brazilian. I'm sure Stacy has enough trouble finding aestheticians without . . . well, you should hurry, dear." I wasn't sure which was more disappointing, not sharing Helen's news or not sharing the good champagne, but she had a point about the aesthetician. That didn't stop me from dawdling outside the room to eavesdrop.

"By the way, Grant sends his regards," Helen said to Miss Irene. She uncorked the champagne with a gentle pop, and I remembered the museum director's upscale wine cellar. "I finally took your advice, Irene! I had a very interesting meeting with my lawyer this morning." The roar of hair dryers swallowed up the rest of Helen's news as business returned to normal.

I climbed the stairs as quickly as I could, which was not very quickly since I had to duck walk to avoid smearing the polish on my toenails. Whatever disaster awaited me was not worth destroying a perfectly good pedicure. Hoping the complimentary pastry buffet had distracted the sisters – and unable to resist snagging a chocolate croissant myself – I checked for them in the changing room first. A trail of lime green, platform espadrilles and fuchsia, pointed toe slingbacks led across the room to where the twins had haphazardly tossed their clothes. Beatrice's clothes were neatly hung from the hooks in her cubby. Her scuffed, white, velcro trainers sat neatly below the shelf. Compared to the twins' booty-booster jeans and bright, silk blouses, Bea's purple and teal nylon windbreaker set looked dull and worn. A couple of the bedazzled rhinestones were missing from the jacket, and the hem on one ankle was coming out.

There was no way Bashful Bea, with her muumuus and 1980s style athleisure wear knew what a Brazilian wax was, let alone would ever consider getting one, I thought. I was certain this was another of the twins' mean jokes.

Peals of laughter bubbled from behind a closed door. My heart broke for poor, trusting, naïve Bea. Sad little gulli-Bea.

The laughter grew louder as the door opened and Stacy exited, shaking her head.

"Is everything . . . erm, okay?" I asked, fearing the worst.

"I'm not sure how much they're relaxing, but maybe a good laugh is just as rejuvenating as a massage," Stacy said.

"They're getting . . . massages?"

"Beatrice wanted to get her legs waxed, but the twins chickened out. Every now and again Beatrice clucks like . . . ." Just then I heard a loud "Puck, puck, puck puKAWK" followed by more laughter.

"Hand to god, they haven't been drinking . . . that much," Stacy said, laughing.

"So, they're getting along?" I still could not believe this change of events.

"Those three are thick as thieves. Laughing and reminiscing

about the old days. All the trouble they used to get into. All the trouble Miss Irene used to get into. The twins are beside themselves. They think Miss Irene was behind Lady Liberty's change of clothing. They're convinced she's back to her old self and that the wedding is back on track."

"And Beatrice?"

Stacy frowned. "I'd say she's cautiously optimistic. But then again, I think that's just her way." Stacy moved closer and lowered her voice. "The hot rumor downstairs is that Miss Irene took a tumble during the caper, and that's how she got that nasty bump on her head."

"Miss Irene was the first person I suspected, too, but . . . . You saw the bump. What do you think?"

"Lightweight, round projectile, approximate inch and a half diameter. Moderate velocity, Most likely fired from a pneumatic source. Unless Lady Liberty defended herself with a pop gun, Miss Irene's not our culprit." Stacy thought for a moment. "Could be an elaborate coverup. Damned Illuminati."

While I do love me a good conspiracy theory, I wasn't ready to go that far.

Yet.

By the time I got back downstairs, Helen – and her champagne – were gone. All Miss Irene would tell me was that Helen had a meeting at the bank. Under her breath she muttered "never understood why she always took him back," and "that man doesn't need a wife, he needs a dog catcher."

Freshly coiffed, and with her makeup and nails done, Miss Irene was anxious to get home. While Pleasant Glen Grille was catering the main course for tonight's family dinner, Miss Irene was making each child's favorite dish, as well. The girls had made double cruncher cookies and Texas sheet cake brownies already, but we – and by "we" I mean "I" – still had to make deviled eggs, green bean casserole, ambrosia salad, fondue, and lime jello salad with cottage cheese.

Stacy had "misplaced" the loaner glasses, and since the girls were getting their chakras aligned, I was enlisted as chauffeur. In her rush to leave, Miss Irene once again tripped over the painted arrow and fell . . .

. . . right into the open arms of Big George.

"Falling for me again, are you dear?" he said.

"Don't flatter yourself, old man," Miss Irene replied. Her words were sharp, but her tone was teasing.

"I would be flattered indeed, my darling, if you were to allow me to assist you." Big George had me swooning. From the way Miss Irene leaned into him, I guessed she was swooning, too.

"Where've you been, George? I tried calling you earlier." Miss Irene looked up at him and batted her eyelashes. I couldn't tell if she was flirting, crying or just trying to focus her eyes.

"Ahhh, yes . . . that. I have something for you." Big George reached into his shirt pocket and pulled out her glasses. He gently slipped the stems over her ears, straightened them, then held her face in his hands and gazed into her eyes.

"But George, how did you . . . ." I recognized the look that passed between the two of them. I knew that, for them, the rest of the world had melted away. It was like the pivotal scene in a romantic movie: time slowed, the camera zoomed in, the background music swelled.

"Reese brought them by the shop . . . ."

Miss Irene stiffened.

The background music gave way to a foreboding silence.

"You were at the shop?" Miss Irene asked. Each word crackled with ice. "You were working?"

"Junior was short handed this morning. I was answering the phone, front office only. Why else would I be dressed like Mr. Rogers?" Instead of the usual navy blue work pants and shirt worn by all the Pleasant Glen Cycles and Motors mechanics, Big George was wearing khakis and a navy blue polo shirt. The edge of a PGC&M logo peeked out from beneath his gray cardigan. And he was wearing sneakers. I had never seen him in anything other than steel-toed work boots.

"There's grease on your cuff."

"Your glasses ... my tools were at my bench and ..." Big George stumbled over his words. "And Junior doesn't have my same standards of cleanliness. I had them fixed in no time and I came straight here ...."

"Your sweater is snagged."

". . . but you were under the dryer, so I went to the VFW and fixed the ball machine before anyone else .... That Reese is a mechanical menace," Big George chuckled, "which makes him one of my best customers." Miss Irene raised one eyebrow, dropping the temperature another 10 degrees. "The *shop's* best customer, I mean, and ...."

"There's mud on your slacks."

Big George cleared his throat. "The pump, for the fountain, over in the square ... it was acting up – all that soap, you know – so I ...."

"You smell of diesel fuel."

"The bucket truck ... the statue ... it was running rough and ... well, I couldn't just ...."

"Inveterate tinkerer. Incorrigible handyman." Miss Irene

spluttered.

"Hmmm, those aren't quite the words the mayor used . . . ."

"Damned meddler."

"That's a little closer."

"George, you promised you'd take it easy. You promised!"

Big George hesitated. I'm sure he knew he was in trouble, but like most men, he didn't know when to stop. "Irene, you can't expect me to change my ways overnight! What more can I do? I'm trying!"

There's a slight chance Miss Irene would have let the matter drop, had not Stacy stuck her head out the salon door right then.

"There you are, Big George! That dryer chair's still not drying. Did the part you ordered come in yet?"

Miss Irene drew herself up to her full five foot three inches. Her nostrils flared. "Duty calls, George. No rest for the wicked. Not that they want to rest, anyway. Not even if they promised." She glared at Big George one last time. "Dinner is at six. Unless you're too busy." Then she carefully stepped over the painted arrow and stomped off towards her car.

Big George knew when he'd been beaten. "If you need me, I'll be in the park. Feeding the birds," he called after her. He sighed and let his shoulders slump. "Dying of boredom."

Chapter 27

Miss Irene had gone too far this time, as far as I was concerned. I ran after her, determined to give her a piece of my mind . . . politely, of course. Her slow, shuffling gait had been replaced by her usual, brisk pace, so by the time I caught up, she had already reached the Lincoln. "It's for his own good, the old fool," I heard her mutter angrily as she stabbed at the driver's side door lock.

Before she could scratch the paint any more than she had already, I took the keys from her, unlocked the door, and held it open for her. "I know you think . . . ."

"I *think* I know you should mind your own damn business!" She grabbed the keys from me and slammed the door shut. I watched, helplessly, as she tore down the street, pushing all eight cylinders to the max. I realized I was going to need something a lot stronger than coffee if I had to spend an afternoon working with her in a small kitchen surrounded by big knives.

Lucky for me The Bar was just around the corner.

Saturdays in Pleasant Glen are usually reserved for shopping trips to River City and chores around the house. Given the nice weather, I was surprised by the number of cars outside The Bar . . . until I heard a band – and Joe – start playing.

When I walked in, Sophia had cornered Bob at the near end of the bar and was complaining loudly. "I told you we should charge cover when he's here. The freeloaders just keep rolling in!" She looked up, pretending not to have recognized me. "Oh, it's just you." She turned back to Bob. "And no comp tickets, either."

I ignored Sophia and took a seat at the other end of the bar. "Beer me, please, Bob," I called.

Sophia, getting the message and gleefully ignoring it, sat next to me and leaned an elbow on the bar. "How's the husband?" she asked solicitously, still trying to get a rise out of me.

"How's the oilman?" I fired back, referring to the Rich Texas Oilman who had recently dumped her for a younger model.

Sophia's hand shot up, and for a moment I thought she had punched me. My head snapped back and I saw stars . . . or at least sparkles . . . caused by the diamond tennis bracelet dangling from her wrist. The ginormous, square cut diamonds were just this side of vulgar and on the far side of stunning.

"Oilman *Junior*, you mean," she said. "He has more hair, more earning potential, and more . . . ahem . . . stamina than his father. And he has a fleet of lawyers working round the clock to keep that gold digger from getting her claws into Senior's money. Junior is loaded, and set to become more loaded. In a word, he's perfect."

Someday I'll learn there's no point in trying to shame the shameless.

Sophia blathered on about her new and very generous beau – his cars, his houses, his planes, his horses, and his . . . ahem . . . stamina. Bob rolled his eyes so much I thought he was going to cause himself brain damage.

"Our romance is still in that new and exciting stage . . ." Sophia gushed.

"You mean *pre*-pre-nup?" Bob suggested.

Sophia gave him a withering look. "I only flew back to Iowa – private jet, of course – to check out The Winkle Pickers." Sophia nodded towards the stage. "Joe says new-wave bluegrass is trending."

In theory, during these mentoring sessions Joe would listen to a group perform and give them feedback. In reality, Joe found it much easier to demonstrate by playing *with* them. Music always came easier than words to Joe. And he loved to create music.

I watched Joe at work, suggesting slight changes, playing, singing, sharing his experience. He was laughing and smiling, clearly enjoying himself, doing what he loved. I could never ask him to give that up. I could never take that away from him. It would kill him.

I thought about Big George. Miss Irene used to call him "the engine whisperer." If it had a motor, Big George could fix it. Now he was sitting on a park bench "waiting to die." And Miss Irene thought that was for his own good?

Liz slid a basket with a burger and fries onto the bar in front of me, interrupting my brooding. "I almost had the kitchen all cleaned up when I heard you come in, Julie. We ran out of the daily special, but I figured you might be hungry," she said.

"I didn't think my stomach was growling *that* loud!"

Liz laughed. "No, dear. I heard it in Joe's music. He and the Turnip Twaddlers, or whatever they're called, were playing "Foggy Mountain Breakdown" at a good clip when all of a sudden Joe kicked it up *another* notch! I don't know how that old piano didn't catch fire!"

"You break a string, you pay for repairs!" Bob shouted towards the stage. Joe and the band had moved on to a spirited rendition of "Roll In My Sweet Baby's Arms."

"You can hear it in the way he plays – the joy, the pride, maybe a dash of showboating for your attention. Just like the old days, Julie," Liz said.

Mary had said almost the same thing. Maybe they were right. Maybe my just being there was enough.

"Hellooooo beautiful." Joe slipped up behind me and kissed that spot on my neck just below my ear . . . as he reached around me to snitch a french fry. Liz's fries give Velma's a good run for their money.

"Are you talking to me or my fries?"

"Definitely you." Joe kissed me again. "And your fries. The rest of us got goulash." He caught Liz's frown and quickly added "and it was good. Very good! But man! Liz's french fries? You're some kind of special."

"Just keep that in mind while you're helping me this afternoon."

Joe started fidgeting. Sophia grinned. I frowned.

"It's just that I didn't know until yesterday that The Winkle Pickers would be in the area. We set up this consult last minute, but then I didn't get in until late last night, and you left early this morning, so I didn't have a chance to run it by you but . . . . I don't think I'd be much help in the kitchen."

"That's a lie and you know it, Joe." Joe was a great cook. Although when we were left unsupervised in a kitchen, it wasn't just the food that heated up. Still, he had promised me he would help me prepare for Miss Irene's dinner.

"Did you notice The Winkle Pickers have a stand up bass?" he asked. I have had a thing for the stand up bass since I watched The Police's video for "Every Breath You Take." Or maybe I just had a thing for The Police. Or maybe just Sting. Regardless, Joe knew the stand up bass was one of my weaknesses and he loved to tease me about it. "If you let me stay now, I'll play the stand up bass for you later."

"You don't play stand up bass," I said, resisting his charm. I may be cheap, but I'm not easy.

"For you? I'd learn." Joe ran his fingertips slowly down my spine, then gently strummed imaginary strings at the small of my back. "For you? Anything."

Apparently I *am* easy.

"Don't make me get the soda gun," Bob warned. He always threatened to douse over-amorous, drunken customers with the soda gun. Sometimes he carried through on that threat.

"Fine! Fine," I said, spinning the bar stool so I could hug Joe. If Bob was going to douse us, I didn't want him to ruin the makeup Stacy had so carefully applied.

"I would have had to make a few adjustments to the menu, anyway," Joe said. "I could not, in good conscience put cottage cheese in lime jello. Everybody knows you're supposed to add pineapple."

Bob shook his head. "Celery and grated carrots."

"Pineapple and cucumbers with a horseradish sauce," Liz corrected.

Sophia turned green. "Gah! This is why I hate the Midwest." Joe had told me Sophia was from a little town along the Mississippi River, so I figured she had her own favorite, equally strange jello salad recipe.

After Joe went back to the band, Liz grilled me about the morning's events. While I could neither confirm nor deny Miss Irene's involvement in the statue dressing affair, I did run Stacy's ballistics report by her.

"What about Muffy?" Sophia asked. "She's the only one in this backwater town with a sense of fashion. Besides me, of course."

"Good point! Where were you last night, and can anyone verify your alibi?"

"Very funny." Sophia's deadpan voice indicated that she found it anything but funny. "As if I'd ever step off the sidewalk in these Ferragamos." She stuck out her legs, which were encased in black, Stella McCartney faux leather slacks, to reveal a pair of pristine, gray satin mules with metallic heels and rhinestone bows. I knew she had nothing to do with the vandalism, but it would have been fun to see her and the mayor face off.

"Besides, I would never have dressed her in that tacky kilt like some Catholic school girl. Those colors clashed horribly with her patina." Sophia thought for a moment. "I'd go with something in navy blue, maybe with a bold pattern to soften those strong features. A one shoulder gown, of course, to show off the torch arm. Something that flows . . . chiffon maybe. An American designer, obviously. Maybe Oscar de la Renta."

I probably should have been more concerned at the amount of thought Sophia put into that, but I had to admit, Lady Liberty would have looked stunning.

❋ ❋ ❋

Before heading home I circled the town square to make sure Big George wasn't still stuck on some park bench. On a whim, I drove down the block to Pleasant Glen Cycles and Motors. The building was dark. They had planned to close early in preparation for the wedding, and Big George wasn't the kind of man to go back on his word.

I cupped my hands against the window and looked in. The usual mix of motorcycles lined the display area. Sitting handlebar to handlebar, upright and attentive on their center stands, headlights facing the street, they reminded me of puppies in a pet store window. Light from the neon advertising signs reflected off them, creating shards of color in the darkness. Back in the corner, Paolo slouched insolently. The dim light from a security fixture emphasized his angularity.

The Scout sat alone in the center of the showroom, out of reach of the lights. She rested on her side stand, front wheel turned back against her body, like a bird tucking its head beneath its wing. Deep shadows drained the luster from her paint.

My heart ached for her. "I'm so sorry, Scout," I sobbed, fogging the window. I wiped away the first wave of tears, then drew a heart in the fog, framing The Scout. J.J. would be all kinds of pissed off Monday when he had to clean the glass, but I didn't care. I leaned my forehead against the window. I blinked back more tears, blurring my vision of The Scout. I could have sworn I saw a shadow drip down the chrome accent on her front fender skirt. It hung, dangling on the upturned trailing edge, then fell to the floor and was swallowed up in the gloom.

Chapter 28

Throughout the afternoon, Miss Irene's children, grandchildren, great-grands, and even a great-great grand or two, gathered at her house as they arrived in Pleasant Glen. "Jockeying for position in the will," Frank said, winking at me. He was spending the night with J.J. and Big George, while the rest of the clan, including Bea and her husband, had taken over the Glen View Inn for the weekend. By six, the grands and beyond left for a pizza party by the pool. The first and second generation sat down to what would have been the rehearsal dinner.

All the leaves had been added to Miss Irene's antique, maple dining table, stretching it the length of the room. Miss Irene sat at the head of the table, flanked by Big George and Frank. Beatrice sat next to her father, along with her husband, the twins and their husbands. Edward sat next to Big George, along with his wife, the other two boys and their wives. J.J., Joe and I sat at a card table which had been added on at the opposite end, in the living room.

"Nearly 60 years old and I'm still sitting at the 'kids' table," J.J. grumbled, taking his place.

Dinner was served buffet style from a couple of banquet tables on loan from St. Cunie's. I was amazed at how smoothly everyone filled their plates and were seated for the blessing. The only time I'd sat down to eat with this many people was in the school cafeteria.

J.J. was unfazed by the crowd. "We've had lots of practice. When we were kids, we always had friends or guys from the shop over for dinner. You know how Miss Irene loves to take in strays. Heck, even after we had left home, our friends would still drop by for a meal."

Conversation was evenly split between catching up on new events and reliving old memories. Each child had at least one semi-embarrassing story told about them. Eventually J.J.'s lack of a "plus one" for dinner was noted as well.

"I'm still trying to make a good impression on her," he explained. "I didn't want you guys to scare her away like you did Debbie Vandenberg!" While the others laughed, J.J. whispered to me "Can you imagine? Dad and Miss Irene are enough to process. I couldn't spring all these people on Vanessa at once." I was still processing the whole idea of my best friend dating my best mechanic, and I wasn't sure how I felt about him wanting to introduce her to his family, either.

As the conversation dwindled, the boys cleared the table – "That's why I married him!" Edward's wife said – and the girls cut the desserts. Frank had brought several cases of champagne for the weekend, and glasses were prepared for toasts. It wasn't quite the same quality as Helen's champagne, but it was still better than what was usually served in Pleasant Glen. "I know a girl in catering at the casino," Frank told me. I didn't ask how well he knew her.

After everyone was settled in again, Frank stood to deliver the first toast. "As I look out over this table, I can't help but think how lucky . . . you kids were to have such a fine group of parents!" This was met with laughter and cat calls.

"Big George, I want to thank you for loving these kids as your own. I couldn't have asked for a better co-father.

"Irene, mother of my children, the biggest mistake I ever made was to let you go. Thank you for instilling in them, and in all of us, a sense of adventure, a zest for life. You encouraged each of us to develop as individuals, to pursue our own passion, to be true to ourselves. From you, we have all learned to live life to its fullest. To love with all our hearts. And to trust in what makes us unique."

While everyone else was clinking glasses, the twins stood to add their own toast.

"To the woman who has been an inspiration to us . . . ." Jan began.

"Who never fails to surprise . . . ." Francine added.

"Who has proven that age is just a number . . . ."

"And that it's never too late to turn over a new leaf . . . ."

"To the bravest of the brave . . . ."

"The daring-est of the daring . . . ."

Miss Irene blushed modestly as her daughters continued their tribute.

"Our sister, Beatrice!"

There was a collective gasp of surprise. Miss Irene's eyebrows nearly shot off her forehead. Beatrice flushed a bright red. I couldn't believe the twins could be so cruel. Before the surprised murmurs died down, Jean reached into the gift bag Francine held and pulled out . . . a familiar looking orange and green plaid kilt.

The table erupted in laughter and cheers.

"How did you know?" Beatrice asked. A huge smile lit her face.

"Are you kidding?" The twins looked at each other as if it were the most obvious thing in the world.

"The coveted Galloping Glennies Glee Club kilt, circa 1962?" asked Jan.

"Glee Club girls were the ginchiest!" said Francine.

"All the girls wanted to be in Glee Club . . ."

"Or at least wear the skirt. Even if they had to raid their sister's closet!"

"And that's why this one . . ."

". . . has one button that doesn't quite match." Francine pointed to one of two brass buttons at the waist of the skirt. From where I sat, the buttons looked identical.

"You could see that from across the street?" Bea sounded astonished.

"Well, that, and the scuff marks on your shoes," Francine admitted.

"And the missing rhinestones on your jacket," Jan added.

Francine shrugged. "I raised four boys. You learn to see the signs."

"But how did you do it, Bea?" Jan asked.

"I raised four girls, who had countless Barbies. You learn to dress stiff-limbed figures. And their dolls."

This set off another round of cheers and toasts. Edward, the second oldest, began singing "For Bea's a Jolly Good Fellow." I took advantage of the mayhem to question J.J.

"What just happened?"

"Like they say, it's the quiet ones you have to look out for. Bea can be just as ornery as the rest of them. She hides it better, is all. Used to get away with murder when we were young, because no one ever suspected her."

Miss Irene sat quietly during the uproar. I watched as her initial look of surprise gave way to a smile. Then, just like had happened before, it was as if someone had flipped a switch. Her smile shriveled until all that was left was an angry frown.

"Beatrice!" Miss Irene's voice, while quiet, had a sharp edge that cut through the frivolity. "What were you thinking? You could have broken your neck! Do you have any idea how dangerous that stunt was?"

The laughter and chatter stopped abruptly. Beatrice bowed her head and clasped her hands like a penitent little girl. "Yes, Mother. I do," she said, speaking softly but firmly. "I could probably find you a dozen charts and graphs to show you how many women my age break a hip every year. After all, I'm an actuary. But what those charts won't tell you is how much fun it was!" She grinned and looked up at her mother. "Even with the hard hat, the knee and elbow pads, the safety harness and tether and the guard-rail step ladder, it was still the most thrilling thing I've done in a long, *long* time.

"Oh, yes, Mother, your little Safety-Bea took every precaution imaginable, because I knew just how dangerous it could be! I've spent my whole life worrying about one thing or another, playing it safe, never straying too far from the straight and narrow. Glee Club instead of basketball, Home Ec instead of Shop. And that was fine by me. But I always wondered if I was missing out on something.

"I always admired you, Mother. You were so brave, so daring, so . . . alive! I lived vicariously through you. I imagined it was me riding off into the sunset on The Scout. That it was me wearing white slacks after Labor Day. But lately . . . I realized that if I don't act now, I may never have the chance. I've seen the charts. I know I'm not going to live forever. I want to make the most of the life I have left. I want to enjoy life . . . safely, of course.

Bea turned to her husband. "Fred, when we get home to Manatee Estates I'm going to get my own golf cart and you're going to teach me to drive it."

"Oh, Bea, I don't know if . . . ."

"Something with a little pep. Or maybe Trey can pep it up for me." Beatrice continued, ignoring her husband. "I'm going to give up armchair yoga and sign up for a Tai Chi class! I may even take up shuffleboard!"

"Beatrice! Only the hotsy-totsy girls play shuffleboard!"

"Oh for heaven's sake, Fred. If I've told you once, I've told you a hundred times, Erma wasn't flirting with you. She has a lazy eye!"

Bea's siblings applauded each new ambition. Miss Irene shook her head. The crease between her eyebrows deepened and her scowl darkened. Finally she stood and slammed her hands on the table, startling everyone.

"Have you all lost your minds?" She spoke in that crisp, no nonsense tone Moms reserve for scolding their children when they're in public. "What are you thinking? Vandalism? Skinny dipping? Shuffleboard? Full-engine overhauls? You're acting like a bunch of irresponsible teenagers, the lot of you!"

She paused and looked around the table again. "It's that damned motorcycle. If it weren't for that hunk of junk, we wouldn't be in this mess to begin with." Her voice dropped to a new level of scary. "I've had enough. I've called the museum. They'll be here Monday morning to haul that two-wheeled troublemaker away. Good riddance to bad rubbish, I say!" The kids started to protest, but she cut them off with a glare.

"And as for all of you . . . it's time to straighten up and fly right. That means no more tinkering, no more trespassing, no more hotsy-totsy! You're all senior citizens, it's time you acted like it!

"Julie will stay and help me clean up. The rest of you can go back to the hotel and think about your actions. Mass begins at 9 tomorrow – sharp. A little more time on your knees wouldn't hurt any of you. Don't. Be. Late."

Miss Irene stormed off, shoving the swinging door so hard it banged against the kitchen wall. We sat watching until the momentum ran out and the door quit moving. Without a word, everyone piled their dessert dishes in the center of the table, then made their way to the front porch to say their hushed goodbyes.

By the time I entered the kitchen, Miss Irene was already elbow deep in sudsy dishwater. I know how cathartic warm dishwater can be, so despite the fact that she was splashing water everywhere, I resisted the urge to redirect her energy. I picked up a dishtowel and started drying and stacking the clean dishes without saying a word.

Our silence was broken by the bump-thump of Frank's wheelchair against the swinging door. Miss Irene looked over her shoulder at him, but didn't stop washing.

"I'm not in the mood, Frank."

"Oh, save your breath to cool your coffee, Irene. I was married to you long enough to know that *you* know you were way out of line in there. And I know that you'll apologize to Beatrice and the rest of them once you calm down." Miss Irene didn't reply, but she didn't throw the knife she was washing at him, either, which I took as a good sign.

"I have a business proposition for you, Irene. Sell me The Scout. Maybe you're right. Maybe if it hadn't been for her, we wouldn't be in this mess in the first place. But she's a part of the family now, and you just don't go around selling off your family." Frank winked at me. "No matter how much you'd like to sometimes."

Miss Irene faced Frank, leaning back against the sink and drying her hands on her apron. "And just who do you think will be able to keep it running, hmmm? I can't sell that motorcycle to you or to Julie, or to anyone in Eastern Iowa . . . heck anyone from here to Timbuktu, for that matter." She threw her hands in the air. "There's only one person who can keep that old relic running, and he has no business tinkering around like that anymore. Don't you see? The museum is the only rational option. The Scout will be well taken care of and George won't have to lift a finger. They'll put it on display behind a plexiglass window, with a little sign out front . . . ."

"And what about George?" Frank cut her off. "Are you going to have him put in a plexiglass case too? Because I'm telling you, Irene, if you take away The Scout, if you make him quit doing what he loves, you'll kill him just as sure as a heart attack would!"

Frank and Irene glared at each other, neither willing to give an inch. The standoff was broken when J.J. poked his head around the door and quietly asked if Frank was ready to go.

"Think about what I said, Irene," Frank said, wheeling backwards through the door. "Think about what you're going to put on *that* little sign."

Chapter 29

Miss Irene and I continued to wash dishes in relative silence, broken only by her occasional muttering or frequent scrub-related splashing. Once he had cleared everything from the dining room table, Joe picked up a towel and dried dishes while I put them away. Joe, being Joe, started to hum absentmindedly. I worried he would annoy the already cross Miss Irene, but she didn't seem to mind. In fact, she was so lost in her own thoughts I wasn't sure she even noticed Joe had taken my place, let alone that he was humming.

I struggled to name Joe's tune. It sounded bluesy – a little somber and melancholy – maybe something I heard him play with Mary and the Blues Shepherds. Just when I thought I had it nailed down, it changed – the tempo sped up, giving it an angry, edgy feel – maybe it was a rock number he picked up from Thunder Pigs. The tune hovered on the edge of my conscience, reminiscent of a song, but not quite a song. It switched up again, becoming plaintive and lonesome – maybe it was something from The Winkle Pickers.

Finally I quit trying to identify the music and let it wash over me, *feeling* the song instead of *thinking* it. As Joe hummed, I felt myself start to relax. It was as if the music were drawing the emotions out of me, helping me vent the anger, frustration and worry of the past week. Somehow he had distilled all those emotions into music, expressing them more eloquently than words could. Joe's tune wasn't just reminiscent of a song, it was reminiscent of feelings.

Joe continued to hum, and I realized that Miss Irene wasn't ignoring him, she was replying to him in her muttering. Or maybe it was the other way around. Their strange, nearly nonverbal conversation seemed to calm her.

Joe hummed. Miss Irene mumbled, *"He's got another think coming!"*

More humming. *"As if I'd . . . ."*

I thought back to when Emily was a toddler and she fought sleep like a warrior princess. At bedtime, I would rock and hum and pat her little bottom, gradually slowing – thinking *she must be asleep by now* – slowing . . . stopping. Then Emily would reach around, put her tiny hand on mine and start patting, letting me know I was on the right track, but not there yet. I'd hum my way through every lullaby, show tune, and Top 40 hit I could think of, until I found just the right melody to help her relax.

Miss Irene's muttering grew softer, the splashing became less frequent, until finally . . . they stopped. She blew out her breath in one long, weary, cleansing sigh that seemed to drain the tension from her body. Without a word, she wrung out the dish cloth and hung it over the faucet. Then she stood on her tiptoes and kissed Joe's cheek. She slowly made her way across the kitchen, and as she passed me she whispered "That one's a keeper." She pushed open the door and looked back at us. "I think I'll turn in. Lock up before you leave, kids."

I waited a few moments after the door had stopped swinging. "Did you hear that? Miss Irene thinks you're a keeper."

"I told you I'd win her over. I just didn't realize I'd get dish pan hands doing it."

Together we finished washing the last of the dishes and got everything cleared away. I sent Joe back to the apartment while I tossed the table cloths and dish towels in the washer, turned off the lights and went upstairs to check on Miss Irene. I was outside her bedroom door when I heard her yell.

"NO! George, no!"

I rushed in and found her sitting up in bed with the blankets twisted around her and tears streaming down her face.

"What have I done?" she sobbed.

"It's okay, Miss Irene. It was just a dream. Just a bad dream. That's all." I sat on the edge of her bed, handing her tissues and rubbing her back, using all the old tricks to calm her that I used to use on Emily when she had a nightmare. I brought her a glass of water and after she took a sip, I asked if she wanted to tell me about it.

"No! Oh, Julie! It was awful. Just awful!" She sniffled and dabbed at her nose. I handed her another tissue that she added to the damp wad in her hands. "Remember when I told you about that day when Big George brought The Scout back after . . . you know, that horrible day at the Tasty Freeze? When Doris accidentally ran over Frank? *Sniff.* When Frank was still in the hospital, but I knew it was all over between us, and Doris had left George and little J.J.? *Sniff.* I told you how George pulled up in that old shop truck with The Scout in the back, and he asked me what I wanted to do with it. And I was so mad, I just wanted to push that motorcycle off the truck, watch it crash to the ground. But I didn't." She shook her head. "I didn't. I asked Big George to teach me to ride, and he did, and we . . . and now . . . ."

Miss Irene swallowed hard and closed her eyes as she recalled her dream. "It was all so real," she whispered. "I was right back there, on that very day. And I was mad. I was *so mad* because it was all *my* fault. I had brought them all together. If it hadn't been for The Scout, if Frank had never found it in that barn . . . . If I had never bought that damn motorcycle and had George fix it up, then Frank and Doris would have never . . . and George and I would have never . . . and George wouldn't be . . . ." She opened her eyes and looked at me. "It was all my fault, and I knew how to save him. I had to get rid of that motorcycle. And I did. I climbed up in the back end of that truck, and I pushed as hard as I could!" She sobbed. "But when I looked over the side, it was George lying in the street! And oh, Julie. I just knew he was . . . ." Miss Irene dissolved in tears.

"What am I going to do," she asked, when she could speak again. "I know he loves that machine, but it's . . . it's a terrible influence – the work, the worries, the . . . everything we've done. All the wild and crazy things . . . . The Scout is a bad influence." She shook her head. "*I'm* a bad influence. It's time we grew up. It's time we started acting our age. What else can I do?"

I thought for a moment. I knew exactly what I wanted to say, but I also knew exactly what Miss Irene would tell me to do with my suggestion – or where I could stick it.

"I don't know, Miss Irene, I don't." I rubbed her back until her breathing steadied. "I remember that story. But I also remember another one. You once told me that everyone hears something different when they listen to The Scout's engine – they hear what they need to hear. Maybe you need to listen to The Scout. What do you think she'd tell you?"

Miss Irene nodded her head, as if considering my suggestion. She held my hand and looked me in the eye, her expression serious. "I think she'd tell me not to eat chocolate cake and drink champagne right before bed. The Scout is a motorcycle, dear, not some mechanical Magic 8 Ball.

"Thank you for your help, dear. I'm feeling much better. Just a spot of indigestion." She patted my hand. "You should get on home to that young man of yours. Don't forget we need to get to church early. There's going to be a crowd."

Chapter 30

Miss Irene's children took her warning seriously and put the fear of God – or maybe the fear of Miss Irene – into *their* children as well. By the time Joe and I arrived at St. Cunegunde's at 8:40, the back six pews on both sides of the aisle were taken up by Miss Irene's progeny – the daughters and their families on the Epistle side, sons and their families on the Gospel side. This displaced the regular parishioners who were used to arriving 10 minutes early, which displaced those used to slipping in right before the Processional, which displaced those used to sneaking in while everyone was still standing for the Gloria. All this seat shuffling resulted in some very non-Christian glares from late-comers who the ushers perp walked farther and farther into the uncharted territory of the front pews.

Those glares were largely wasted on the interlopers, who were too distracted to notice much of anything, including the Mass itself. Miss Irene's grandchildren had their hands full trying to discipline their children, who were unaccustomed to arriving at Mass so early and were distracted by the presence of their cousins. The grands also had to contend with their parents, who were unaccustomed to arriving at Mass so early and were distracted by the presence of their grandchildren.

All of them were distracted by the absence of Miss Irene.

Despite her order that everyone be at and early for Mass, Miss Irene herself had not yet arrived by the First Reading. Frank, Big

George and Helen were missing as well.

"Pssst. Julie! Pssssssst," Beatrice whispered loudly to me from across the aisle and one pew back during the Responsorial Psalm. "Where are they?" Dr. Haselmayer, across the aisle and one row up, frowned at me. I mouthed a silent "I'm sorry" to him before turning to Bea, raising my hands, palms up and shrugging, in the universal sign of "I don't know."

"What do you mean, 'you don't know'?" loudly whispered Miss Irene's youngest son Henry, who was two rows back and directly behind me. Mrs. Bensmiller, two rows ahead of me at the far end of the pew, turned and gave me a withering look. I quickly ducked my head and said a prayer for forgiveness before turning around to Henry Junior, who was seated behind me and in front of his father. I motioned for him to lean forward.

"Tell your dad Miss Irene was already gone by the time we left home," I whispered. Henry Junior turned towards the aisle so he could pass the message to both his father and Aunt. Henry Junior's son took advantage of his father's momentary distraction by trying to escape and join his cousins across the aisle. Without looking, Henry Junior grabbed his son by the collar and placed him back in his seat. Henry Junior sighed and turned back around to me, never loosening his grip on the nape of his son's neck.

"They want you to ask J.J." he semi-whispered.

I leaned forward in the pew and looked across Joe, Emily, Trey, Michael, Steve and Vanessa to where J.J. was sitting. He – and most of the congregation – had heard the entire conversation up to this point, and had already turned towards Henry. "The dads were gone by the time I got up."

Before I had a chance to sit back, Emily leaned forward. Her face was pale, and she looked worried. "I don't think Gramma Helen came home at all last night!" I heard a gasp and looked up to see the entire Messenger family, who took up most of the row ahead of us, staring at Emily, their mouths gaping.

The collection that day was eclipsed only by that of Christmas and Easter. Parishioners who had surreptitiously pulled out their cell phones while reaching for their wallets, felt obligated to put something in the plate, even if it was a 20 dollar bill. Gossipy texts were sent skyward along with prayers for the missing. Of the two, the prayers had a better chance of being answered, as cell reception was poor inside St. Cunie's brick walls.

Things settled down as Mass entered the home stretch. There were a few yelps as some of the kids – of all ages – tried to see who could squeeze hands the hardest during the Our Father. Many parishioners who had been unsettled by the new seating arrangement chose to dine and dash, rather than returning to their pews after Communion. During the recessional, Father Martin nearly ran over the cross bearer in his haste to reach the narthex and check his phone for the latest news.

Out in the parking lot, everyone compared messages. Beatrice had received a short text from Miss Irene: *Special dispensation.*

"Special dispensation? What does that even mean?" Beatrice asked, staring at her phone. "If we had tried that when we were kids . . . ."

Frank had texted J.J.: *Sinners saved? I need a ride to Irene's.*

"At least he still has his sense of humor," J.J. said. "But where is Dad?"

My text was from Helen: *@ Irene's. Where R U?*

Taking these texts as proof of life, we decided there was

nothing left to do but stick with the schedule and hope for more details later. The bulk of our party returned to the hotel to change from their church/wedding clothes to something more appropriate for an outdoor family reunion. I returned home to report for duty.

Helen was in Miss Irene's back yard waiting for me and supervising the last of the party preparations. A crew from the rental store had set up the tent and was now arranging round tables and chairs. Bob was setting up a minibar in one corner. The caterers were carrying roasters and platters into the garage.

"Where were you last night, Helen?" I asked. "Emily said you didn't come home!"

"Last night?" Helen giggled joyfully. "I had dinner with Grant! And then some old friends invited us to an . . . event . . . at the casino. There was champagne and dancing and . . . did I mention champagne?" Helen giggled again. "Time just slipped away, and we decided it would be prudent to get rooms at the hotel. Oh, Julie! It was magical! To think, after so many years . . . ." Helen had a far off look in her eyes. While I was happy that she was happy, I really didn't want any details about her magical night with Grant.

"But where's Miss Irene?" I asked.

"Not to worry dear. She told me she didn't sleep well last night and was running behind this morning. I said I'd keep an eye on things until you got here."

"Do you think I should go in and . . . ."

"Oh, no. She's fine, just fine. Trust me."

Before I could press Helen for details, Trey joined us.

"Dad said he had an errand to run for Aunt Bea, so I brought Grampa Frank over. He's in the house watching football. He sent me out here to help you."

"Did he happen to say where he was this morning?" I asked.

"He said something to Dad about the early bird special at the casino and how 'you only live once, but if you do it right, once is enough'."

"The casino? Helen, did you . . . ."

"Hmmm, small world," Helen said. "Trey, would you mind helping me with the centerpieces? They're not . . . centered. Julie, will you excuse us, dear?"

I thought the centerpieces looked perfectly centered, but before I could say anything, I was distracted by J.J. driving the shop truck into the yard.

"Some hair-brained scheme of Beatrice's," he said after parking the truck under the old oak tree. I had to admit, the shiny red truck did look nice there under the yellow and orange leaves. I figured if we put a couple of Helen's centerpieces on the back end, maybe no one would notice.

"We've got bigger problems than the truck, Julie." J.J. motioned for me to come closer, then whispered, "The Scout is missing."

"What do you mean, *missing*?"

"I mean, I went to the shop to get the truck and when I went in to get the keys from my office, The Scout was . . . missing."

"And your dad is . . .?"

"Missing."

"You don't think he . . .?"

"The trailer was still there, and I haven't been able to get her to even turn over, so . . . ." J.J. shrugged. "But if anyone could get her to start, Dad could."

I looked around the yard while I tried to make sense of things.

Family and a few friends were starting to arrive. "Maybe the museum's schedule changed. I'll go in and ask Miss Irene."

"There you are, Julie!" Helen seemed to materialize out of thin air as soon as I mentioned Miss Irene's name. "I need your help with the, um . . . J.J., isn't that Vanessa? And who's that with her? *Gary*? What's he doing here?"

While J.J. welcomed Vanessa, Gary headed straight for his mother.

"Gary, darling. What a pleasant . . . surprise." Helen said, accepting his kiss on her cheek. "But what are you doing here?"

"I'm your plus one, Mother, remember?" Gary was wearing a charcoal suit, silver shirt and a black and gray subtly checked silk tie. Combined with his ever so slightly salt and pepper hair, he was GQ cover-worthy. He was also completely overdressed for a casual family reunion.

"But you said you couldn't come, so I invited . . . ." Helen hesitated.

"My schedule changed," Gary smiled charmingly. "Couldn't leave my best girl unchaperoned. Or best girls, as the case may be. Flying solo, Jules?" he asked, erasing his charm.

"Not exactly." Joe wrapped his arm around my waist. "Looks like someone missed the 'wedding canceled' memo."

Gary glanced at the other guests, most of whom were wearing jeans. His grin took on an ornery, lopsided tilt. He loosened his tie, achieving an end-of-the-night, drunken groomsman look that made him even more sexy. I noticed all four of Beatrice's daughters staring starry-eyed at him and ignoring their husbands.

"That explains a lot," Gary said, looking Joe over. "I was wondering where you'd parked your tractor." I thought Joe's black Pleasant Glen Cycles and Motors t-shirt and jeans made him look very rock star rebel, but there was no denying his farm-boy roots.

"You can't just switch your 'plus one' status like that, dear, and you know it." Helen redirected Gary's attention. "What are you really doing here?"

Joe kissed my cheek to mark his territory, then excused himself to finish setting up the sound system.

"Mother, what is going on?" Gary's expression grew serious. "Dad said you've filed for divorce."

"I'm merely giving your father what he has asked for so many times over the years. Before I left Florida, he told me he had met a young woman and fallen in love. Again."

"Yes, but we both know he doesn't mean it. He never does. Give him a month or two. He'll get over it and then you two can patch things up."

Helen smiled and shook her head. "Not this time, dear. I've realized I'm not getting any younger – none of us is, darling. I want a chance at happiness."

"But Dad said he's selling the business. He said he wants to move in with *me*! Mother! You can't do this to me!"

"Oh now you're just being melodramatic. And so is your father. Richard will get a more than equitable settlement from the business. And I've found a buyer for your house here in Pleasant Glen who is willing to overlook the . . . irregularities in the paperwork your father filed. As for your father's living arrangements, the two of you will have to work things out. Although if I were you, I'd think twice if he asks you to co-sign anything for him." I admired the brusquely efficient manner Helen dealt with the situation. I had always thought

Gary inherited his business acumen from his father, but now I realized I had misjudged his mother.

"Ah ha! It's good to find someone else around here with a sense of style. Besides Lady Liberty, of course," Sophia said as she sidled up to Gary. She slipped her arm through his, more to improve her balance than as a show of affection. Today's impractical but fashionable footwear was a pair of Gianvito Rossi, python, pointed toe, spike heeled, tall boots. I'm sure she considered the brown suede Prada mini skirt and striped cashmere sweater she was wearing classified as "casual wear," but she and Gary were easily the best dressed couple in all of Pleasant Glen that afternoon. Beatrice's four daughters all sighed, although I'm not sure if it was in envy of Sophia's outfit, or her proximity to Gary.

"Sophia? What are you . . . ." I sputtered. "Does no one understand the concept of 'plus one'?"

"Oh, relax, Miss Manners. Frank invited me."

"Frank? But when? How . . . .?"

"I met him at the casino last night. I'm stuck here for a couple of days until Oilman Junior regains control of the corporate jet." Sophia made a little "tsk" of frustration and shifted her weight to one leg, sinking a heel into the soft dirt. "Frank is quite the high roller. And so charming. You were there with him, weren't you," she said to Helen. "Along with . . . ."

"Speaking of Frank," Helen interrupted, "I believe he's trying to get everyone's attention."

Frank was on Miss Irene's back porch, tapping on a microphone Joe handed him. Everyone migrated towards the house.

"Miss Irene has asked me to say a few words," Frank

announced, "and as you know, she's not the type to take no for an answer." We all chuckled and nodded in agreement. "As I look out over all my children and grandchildren, great-grandchildren and beyond, I can't help but think . . . what a fine lookin' bunch you all turned out to be. Good thing you all took after my side of the family!" Frank glanced down at his watch while he waited for the laughter to die down.

"I know we had all hoped to witness the union of two very special people today. Two people who share a rare and precious bond. But the fact is, sometimes things don't work out the way you want them to. When it comes right down to it, there's not much in this life we can control . . . not even the people we love. Especially not them. The best we can do is love them the way they are, support them, and hope they come to their senses." Frank paused and looked at his watch again.

I leaned over to J.J. and whispered "Does it seem like he's stalling?"

J.J. nodded. "Maybe his age is catching up with him. A touch of dementia?"

"So you won't be witnessing a wedding ceremony today, but . . . ." Frank's cell phone started playing "Great Balls of Fire." He checked it then continued. "We won't be witnessing a wedding ceremony today, but what is a ceremony? Just so much pffft."

Something else caught my attention while Frank was talking. I cocked my head and concentrated on the far-off hum of a motorcycle engine. There was something familiar, something honey-smooth and sultry about the sound. Something content, something satisfied.

"Is that . . . ." I looked at J.J.

"Point is, we won't have a wedding ceremony today because . . . ." I heard Frank say.

J.J. looked at me, and we both spoke at the same time. "The Scout!"

"Because I married these crazy kids last night!" Frank shouted as the motorcycle appeared around the side of the garage. Miss Irene parked behind the shop truck, then pulled off her helmet and sat beaming at her family. Big George, sitting in the sidecar, pulled his goggles up over his helmet and waved to us.

"Ladies and gentlemen, I present to you at long last, Irene and George Monroe. George would you please kiss the bride?" Cheers from the crowd drowned out Frank's words, but George kissed her anyway.

Chapter 31

I thought the cheering was loud when The Scout drove up, but all heck broke loose when Miss Irene kissed her grinning groom. I pulled Helen aside during the pandemonium.

"So, you went to an 'event' at the casino with some old friends?" I asked, accusingly.

Helen eyes twinkled. "Don't be angry with us, dear. You know Irene. Once she gets an idea in her head there's no stopping her. Oh, Julie! It was wonderful! Frank performed the ceremony, Grant and I were witnesses, and the champagne! Oh, my!" The grandchildren were passing out glasses of champagne now, and everyone drank a toast to the happy couple. "Frank gets quite the VIP treatment at the casino. We had the best rooms in the house!" Helen giggled. "And it was all *on the house*, after he hit that big jackpot! Who knew you could win so much money betting on a little marble!"

"Mother! This is serious!" Gary cornered his mother once again. He had taken off his jacket and rolled up his sleeves, pushing his sex appeal off the charts. Sophia still clung to his arm and Bea's daughters were circling closer. "What are you going to do about Dad?"

"I'm sorry, dear, but he's *your* problem now. I'm sure you two will work something out." Sophia led Gary away toward the bar, where the champagne corks were popping like popcorn.

"But what about *you*, Helen?" I asked. "What are you going to do? Where are you going to live?"

"Me? Why I'm moving back to Pleasant Glen, of course." Helen sipped her champagne, then grinned slyly. "I bought your house . . . and Richard's share of the business." Helen finished her drink and sighed contentedly. "If you'll excuse me, I think I should find Grant and take advantage of the buffet. This champagne really is delightful!"

I had a million questions for Helen, but the crowd of well wishers surrounding the newlyweds had nearly dispersed, so I went to add my congratulations.

"Thank you, Julie," Big George whispered as he hugged me. "I don't know what you said to her, but thank you."

Miss Irene's hug was tighter, longer and involved a few more tears.

"All right, Miss Irene, what gives?" I asked, after she let me go.

"I knew you were right, Julie. I didn't want to admit it to you, or even to myself, but I knew you were right. I had to talk to The Scout. I slipped out the front door as soon as you left and let myself into the shop. Oh, my! She looked so sad sitting there in the darkness – that damn Moto Guzzi leering at her from the corner like some slick-haired hoodlum. And you know what she said to me, Julie?" I shook my head and sniffed back a tear. "Not a damn thing, because she's a motorcycle, not some mechanical Magic 8 Ball!" Miss Irene threw back her head and laughed.

"I realized it was never about what she said or what I heard, it was about what I *felt* when I was riding. And sitting there on that worn leather saddle, all the memories came rushing back. Not just the memories of riding The Scout, but all the memories of our life together. Big George and I have lived life to the fullest, Julie. Sometimes maybe we lived life to overflowing! I'm not ready to give that up, and neither is he. But he was willing to try, just to please me. I can't imagine my life without him, Julie. And I can't imagine a life of just . . . existing, with or without him. I'm a lucky woman."

"Darn tootin'!" Big George said, wrapping his arms around her. "You're the woman I want to grow old with. It just doesn't have to happen so soon!"

Beatrice maneuvered Frank's wheelchair across the grass to where we were standing. "Cutting it a little close there, weren't you, Irene?" he asked. "Lucky for you I'm a natural orator."

"You're a natural something, Frank." Miss Irene hugged her ex-husband. "Thanks again for all your help – today and last night."

"Couldn't let that twenty-dollar minister license go to waste! You know, they're thinking of hiring me on at the casino. Apparently that jump-suited Elvis impersonator was a fraud. I may not have his moves," Frank gestured to the wheelchair, "but I still have style. Speaking of which, where's that Sophia? She's a pip! And those legs!"

The thought of Frank and Sophia together both amused and frightened me. "I hate to be the voice of reason, Frank, but Sophia already has a boyfriend. Or two."

"That's the way I like 'em," he said, winking at me. "Keeps 'em from getting too clingy!"

I guess that Beatrice must be used to her father's antics by now. She shook her head and flagged down a grandchild to escort Frank to the buffet.

"Everything turned out wonderfully, Mother," Bea said shyly.

"It did, Beatrice. It did indeed. Thank you, dear." Miss Irene pulled Bea in for a warm embrace, not at all like the stiff, awkward greeting they had exchanged at the airport. "But if you ever pull another stunt like you did with the Statue of Liberty, I'm grounding you!"

"How about if I ask you to help me?" Bea grinned.

Miss Irene hesitated. "We'll see," she whispered. "Now, would someone please tell me why in the world the shop truck is parked back here?"

"It's all Bea's fault! She made me do it!" J.J. pointed an accusing finger at his newly official step-sister. I wondered how many times this same scene had played out when they were younger.

"Don't you remember when we were kids and we would go to the drive-in and we'd all pile in the back of the truck to watch the movie?" Beatrice asked Miss Irene and Big George. "That's where we were, watching 'South Pacific,' when you two kissed for the first time! I thought it might bring back memories . . . remind you of how you fell in love."

Miss Irene and Big George gazed at each other and smiled.

"Oh, my little 'Bali Ha'i' Bea," Miss Irene shook her head, "that was . . . ."

"That was very thoughtful, dear." Big George interrupted.

"But there's more! Wait right here!" Bea clapped excitedly and hurried toward the porch where Joe was sitting at an electric keyboard.

"That wasn't your first kiss, was it?" I asked Miss Irene when Bea was out of earshot.

"Not even close," Miss Irene said, giggling.

"But it was one of the first after I convinced her to quit wasting her time on that banker from up by Danesburg," Big George said.

Miss Irene snorted. "Floyd cared more about my share of

227

Father's bank than he cared for me. Can you imagine? He wanted me to get rid of The Scout. Said it was unseemly for a woman of my position to be riding a motorcycle and cavorting with hoodlums!"

"Ah, Floyd was just jealous of all the time we spent together." Big George leaned closer to me and added in a stage whisper: "She was relentless in her pursuit of me."

"I swear, I was in the shop nearly every day that summer. The Scout developed a seemingly endless set of problems, and of course George was the only one who could fix them. I finally realized they were a package deal and just gave in!"

"So The Scout intervened that time, too?" I asked.

Miss Irene laughed. "She may be a *little* magical after all!"

Up on the porch, Joe started playing another of his "reminiscent of a song-songs" while Beatrice signaled for everyone to quiet down.

"It's been a while since I last worked as a wedding singer," Joe said, "but there are some women you just can't say no to . . . and this back yard seems to be full of them! A wise man once told me there's very little a man won't do for the woman he loves. Apparently that holds true for daughters and their mothers, too. Isn't that right, Beatrice?"

Bea stepped to the front of the porch and smiled at Miss Irene and Big George as Joe began playing the introduction to "Some Enchanted Evening." Joe, knowing how to cater to a crowd, let Bea handle most of the vocals, chiming in for the occasional harmony. Bea's voice sent shivers down my spine. She had a rich, soulful sound that reminded me of those great female singers who performed with the big bands of the 1930s and 40s. I looked at Miss Irene in surprise.

"That's our little Glee Bea," Miss Irene said proudly. "You know, they cast her as Nellie Forbush in the PG Players performance of *South Pacific* when she was still in high school!"

Bea's daughters rushed the stage when the song ended, followed closely by the rest of the family. Joe looked out over the crowd, searching for me. When he caught my eye, I saw his megawatt smile shine even brighter. He was clearly in his element – an element with plenty of room for me.

"Helen told me she's moving back to Pleasant Glen," Miss Irene said, as we watched Francine and Jean fuss over Bea.

"Yes, but I don't understand how. I mean, the house . . . the business? Where did she get the money?"

"Didn't you know, dear? Her great-aunt left a very large estate – in Helen's name only! Richard has been living on an allowance all these years."

I thought I knew my mother-in-law well, but she was just full of surprises.

"The big question is what are *you* going to do now?" Miss Irene asked.

"What do you mean?"

"With your house squared away, your divorce can finally proceed. And you can get on with your life." Miss Irene nodded at Joe.

"Oh!" I said with genuine surprise. "We've been stuck in a holding pattern for so long, I haven't let myself think about the future . . . much. I love him, but we live such different lives." Joe was slowly making his way to the edge of the crowd, but it seemed there was always one more person who wanted to shake his hand, or take a selfie with him. "It's going to be a real adventure combining them, isn't it?"

"It took Big George and me nearly 50 years to figure it out." Miss Irene took my hand in hers. "I'm not the one you should ask for advice." Joe finally broke free and was striding toward us, his smile growing bigger with each step. Miss Irene slipped the key to The Scout into my hand. "Just have her home by morning, dear. You might not be the only one who needs advice."

Miss Irene pointed to table at the near side of the tent, where J.J. and Vanessa sat sharing a piece of chocolate wedding/reunion/wedding cake. Earlier in the week, Vanessa had stabbed my hand with her fork when were sampling cake for Steve and Michael's reception. I should have known better than to sneak a bite, but *still*. And here she was *voluntarily* sharing – *chocolate* cake, no less – with J.J. Maybe this *was* more serious than I realized. But the best part was, instead of that queasy, nervous feeling I usually got when I thought of the two of them together, all I felt was happy.

Miss Irene held her arms out to Joe. "Come here, you!" She hugged him and gave him a peck on his cheek. "Thank you, Joe. For everything."

"My pleasure, Ma'am. Bea has quite a set of pipes! Did she inherit that from you?"

"Oh, my no. That she really did get from her father. I can't carry a tune in a bucket with two handles."

Back on the porch/stage, Bea's daughters had joined her for a spirited, acapella version of "Wash That Man Right Outa My Hair." They all had inherited Bea's singing ability. Miss Irene joined the rest of their audience, leaving Joe and I alone.

"I take it you didn't spend all afternoon with The Winkle Pickers," I said, hugging him.

"I'm so sorry, Julie. It seems like even when we are together we're . . . not. I promise I'll make it up to you. In fact, I have a couple ideas that could mean less time on the road, less time apart."

"It's alright, honey. It's all part of who you are, and I never want you to change. I'll always be your biggest fan."

"You know, that song reminded me of this waitress I once knew." Joe put his arms around my waist and started swaying as he half sang, half spoke. "I looked out across the crowded bar, and somehow I knew – I knew even then – I had to make you my own." Joe kissed that spot just below my ear and I went weak in the knees. "Now that I've found you – again – I'll never let you go. No matter how long I have to wait."

"About that . . . I have a couple things to tell you. But first," I held up The Scout's key and shook it, "how 'bout a ride?"

Joe raised one eyebrow. "Not quite what I had in mind, but I'm game." We walked to the motorcycle hand in hand. "What should we do about that?" he asked, pointing to a "Just Married" sign that had been hung on the sidecar.

I thought about Vanessa and J.J., Helen and Grant, Frank and – heaven help us – Sophia.

"We'd better keep it," I said. "You never know who might need it next."

ACKNOWLEDGEMENT

This project took considerably more time than I expected. I think it was worth it in the end, and I hope you will too. Thank you to my family and friends who continued to encourage me and who didn't give up on me or let me give up on myself. Special thanks to Scott, Gabby and Max for their patience and understanding.

Along the way I asked a lot of people a lot of questions. Sometimes I even took their advice! (And sometimes story-telling got in the way.) Thank you to Alex, Luke, Scott, Teresa, Lynn and more for your insights.

Thank you to those brave souls who read early drafts and humored me as I mused aloud, working out plot points and ideas, including Kendra, Ginny, Karen and David.

I hope you enjoy reading the adventures of Julie and friends as much as I enjoy writing about them. If I made you laugh or cry ... or both, please recommend my books to friends or leave a brief review wherever possible.

Let's do this again soon!

ABOUT THE AUTHOR

Joanne Salemink

Joanne Salemink is a former journalist, high school English teacher and stay-at-home-mom. She hasn't decided what she wants to be when she grows up, but is leaning toward writer or superhero. She likes happy endings, good stories, laughing until someone snorts and living in Eastern Iowa with her husband and two grown children. Joanne randomly blogs about all that and more at Sandwichmomonwry.blogspot.com.

BOOKS BY THIS AUTHOR

Scout's Honor

Julie Westbrook's mid-life crises are piling up faster than credit card rewards on Black Friday. Just when things seem to be at their bleakest, she meets Miss Irene, an ageless octogenarian with a penchant for pole dancing and a vintage Indian Scout motorcycle. Armed with a sense of humor, courage she forgot she had, and an unfortunate nice-girl streak she can't shake, Julie reignites a romance and kick-starts a new life.

Humor. Drama. Romance ... and a motorcycle.

Made in the USA
Monee, IL
17 September 2022

13325146R00134